Deciding not to believe him, she looked past his shoulder to the door. "How did you get into my office without Pauline announcing you?"

He shrugged. "I told her she didn't have to bother. I like announcing myself. Besides, she was packing up to leave, and she told me to tell you that she would see you Monday morning."

Hunter glanced at her watch. She hadn't realized it was so late. That meant they were alone, and that wasn't a good thing right now with her present frame of mind. The best thing to do was to send him packing. Picking up the manila folder off her desk, she offered it to him. "Here's what you came for."

Tyson moved toward her with calm, deliberate strides, and when he came to a stop directly in front of her, she tried ignoring the sparks going off inside her. Instead of accepting the folder, he reached out and brushed the tips of his fingers across her cheek. "That's not what I came for, Hunter. This is."

And before she could draw her next breath, he leaned in and captured her mouth with his.

Dear Reader,

They are back!

I love writing about men who defiantly reject the notion of falling in love. Men who honestly believe there is no woman out there who has the ability to tame their wild heart.

When I began writing about the Steele family, introducing them in my first book, *Solid Soul*, where my readers got to meet Chance Steele, I knew these men would be special. When I had accomplished the feat of marrying off all the Steeles in Charlotte, North Carolina, I gleefully turned my attention to their rambunctious cousins who lived in Phoenix. They are the ones known as the "Bad News" Steeles.

There are six brothers. So far we've married off Galen, Eli and Jonas. Now, in *Possessed by Passion*, you'll get to see how Tyson Steele puts up a bitter fight until the end. Like his brothers, Tyson thinks he knows how to play the game and win. However, an old flame by the name of Hunter McKay shows him it's not always a game. Once in a while, it's all about possession. And when you throw passion in the mix, a lot of things can happen.

Thank you for making the Steeles a very special family. I look forward to bringing you more books of endless love and red-hot passion.

Happy reading!

Brenda Jackson

BRENDA JACKSON

POSSESSED BY PASSION

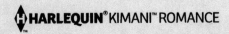

HARLEQUIN® KIMANI™ ROMANCE

Recycling programs
for this product may
not exist in your area.

ISBN-13: 978-0-373-86441-6

Possessed by Passion

Printed in U.S.A.

Brenda Jackson is a *New York Times* bestselling author of more than one hundred romance titles. Brenda married her childhood sweetheart, Gerald, and has two sons. She lives in Jacksonville, Florida. She divides her time between family, writing and traveling. Email Brenda at authorbrendajackson@gmail.com or visit her on her website at brendajackson.net.

Books by Brenda Jackson

Harlequin Kimani Romance

Steele Family

Irresistible Forces
Intimate Seduction
Hidden Pleasures
Possessed by Passion
A Steele for Christmas
Private Arrangements

In Bed with the Boss
Just Deserts
The Object of His Protection
Temperatures Rising
Bachelor Untamed
Star of His Heart
Bachelor Unleashed
In the Doctor's Bed
Bachelor Undone
Bachelor Unclaimed

Visit the Author Profile page at
Harlequin.com for more titles.

To the man who will always and forever
be the love of my life, Gerald Jackson, Sr.

To all my readers who waited patiently on another novel
about those "Bad News" Steeles,
this one is especially for you.

And to my readers who gave me their love, support and
understanding as I endured a difficult time in my life,
I appreciate you from the bottom of my heart.

Though your beginning was small,
yet your latter end would increase abundantly.

Chapter 1

"I understand you became an uncle last night, Tyson. Congratulations."

Tyson Steele glanced over at the man who'd slid onto the bar stool beside him. Miles Wright was a colleague at the hospital where they both worked as surgeons. "Thanks. How did you know?"

"It was in this morning's paper. Quite the article."

Tyson shook his head as he took a sip of his drink. Leave it to his mother, Eden Tyson Steele, to make sure the entire city knew about the birth of her first grandchildren. Twins. A boy and a girl that represented a new generation of Steeles in Phoenix. Everyone was happy for his brother Galen and his wife, Brittany, but his mother was ecstatic beyond reason. Within the past three years, not only had three of her six die-hard bachelor sons gotten married, but as of last night she also had a grandson and granddaughter to boast about.

He wondered if Galen was aware of the article in this morning's paper since he hadn't mentioned it when Tyson had spoken to him earlier. Knowing their mother, Tyson wouldn't be surprised if the announcement appeared in the *New York Times* next. A former international model whose face had graced the covers of such magazines as *Vogue*, *Cosmo* and *Elle*, his mother still had connections in a lot of places and had no shame in using them.

Miles's beeper went off and with an anxious sigh he said, "Need to run. I got an emergency at the hospital."

"Take care," Tyson told his colleague, who moved quickly toward the exit door. He then glanced around. Notorious was a popular nightclub in Phoenix, but not too many people were here tonight due to the March Madness championship basketball game being held in town. Usually, on any given night, Tyson could have his pick of single women crowding the place, but not tonight.

His brothers had tried talking him into attending the game with them, but he'd declined after his team had been eliminated in the previous round. It didn't matter one bit when they'd laughed and called him a sore loser. So what if he was.

Tyson took another sip of his drink and checked his watch. It was still early, but he might as well call it a night since it seemed he would be going home alone, which wasn't how he'd envisioned spending his evening. Taking some woman to bed had been at the top of his agenda. Scoring was the name of the game. Women hit on him and he hit on women. No big deal. It was the lay of the land. His land anyway.

He stood to leave at the same time the nightclub's door swung open and three women walked in. Three good-looking women. He sat back down, thinking that maybe the night wouldn't be wasted after all.

Not to be caught staring, he turned around on the bar stool. The huge mirror on the wall afforded him the opportunity to check out the women without being so obvious. Good, he noted. No rings. That was the first thing he looked for since he didn't believe in encroaching on another man's territory. Tyson figured it must be his lucky night when they were shown to a table within the mirror's view. The women were so busy chatting that they didn't realize he was checking them out.

For some reason his gaze kept returning to one of the women in particular. She looked familiar and it took a second or two before it hit him just who she was.

Hunter McKay.

Damn. It had been years. Eighteen, to be exact. She had been two years behind him in high school, and of all the girls he'd dated during that time, she was the only one with whom he hadn't been able to score. She'd had the gall to ask for a commitment before giving up the goods, and unlike some guys, who would have lied just to get inside her panties, he'd told her the very same thing then that he was telling women now. He didn't do commitments. His refusal to make her his steady girl had prompted her to end things between them after the first week. It had been the first time a Steele had ever been shot down. For months his brothers had teased him, calling Hunter "the one who got away." He frowned, wondering why that memory still annoyed him.

When he'd returned to Phoenix after medical school he'd heard she attended Yale to fulfill her dream of being an architect. After college she had made her home in Boston and returned to town only occasionally to visit her parents. Their paths had never crossed until tonight.

He'd also heard she had gotten married to some guy she'd met while living in Boston. So where was her ring? She could be getting it cleaned, resized or...maybe she was no longer married. He couldn't help wondering which of those possibilities applied.

Hunter had been a striking beauty back then and she still was. It had been that beauty that had captured his interest back in the day and was doing so now. It didn't appear as if she'd aged much at all. She still had that young-girl look, and those dimples in both cheeks were still pretty damn pleasing to the eyes.

The shoulder-length curly hair had been replaced with a short natural cut that looked good on her, and he couldn't help it when his gaze lingered on her lips. He could still remember the one and only time he'd kissed her. It has been way too short, yet oh so sweet.

He felt an ache in his groin and didn't find it surprising since it was a familiar reaction whenever he saw a beautiful woman. But it was Hunter who was affecting him, not the other two women. He remembered them from high school as well, but had forgotten their names.

What he did recall was that they had been Hunter's best friends even back then.

"Ready for another drink, Doc?"

He glanced up at Tipper, who'd been the bartender at Notorious for years. "Not yet, but do me a favor."

Tipper grinned. "As long as it's legal."

"It is. Whatever drinks those three ladies are having, I want them put on my tab."

Tipper glanced over at the table where the women sat and nodded. "No problem. I'll let their waiter know."

"Thanks."

Tipper walked off and Tyson's gaze returned to the mirror. At that moment Hunter threw her head back and laughed at something one of the women said. He'd always thought she had a sensuously shaped neck, flawless and graceful. He'd looked forward to placing a hickey right there on the side of it. It was the place he would brand all the girls in high school who'd gone all the way with him. It had been known as the Mark of Tyson. But Hunter had never gotten that mark. What a pity.

His cell phone pinged with a text message and he pulled his phone out of his jacket to read his brother Mercury's message. *My team is up four. Be ready to celebrate later tonight.*

Tyson clicked off the phone and rolled his eyes. *When hell freezes over,* he thought. If his brothers thought he was a sore loser, then Mercury could be an obnoxious winner, and Tyson wanted no part of it tonight. After returning the phone to his jacket, he let his gaze return to the mirror and to Hunter. He couldn't help but smile when he made up his mind about something. Her name might be Hunter but tonight he was determined to make her his prey.

Hunter McKay appreciated sharing this time with her two best friends from high school—Maureen Santana, whom everyone fondly called Mo, and Kathryn Elliott, whose nickname was Kat. Both had been bridesmaids in her wedding and because they'd kept in touch over the years, they'd known about her rocky marriage and subsequent divorce from Carter Robinson. Mo, a divorcée herself, thought Hunter had given Carter far too many chances to get his act together, and Kat, who was still holding out for Mr. Right, had remained neutral until Carter had begun showing his true colors.

"Here you are, ladies," the waiter said, placing their drinks in front of them. "Compliments of the gentleman sitting at the bar."

Their gazes moved past the waiter to the man in question. As if on cue, he swiveled around in his seat and flashed them a smile. Hunter immediately felt a flutter in the pit of her stomach, a flutter that should have been forgotten long ago. But just that quickly, after all these years, it had resurfaced the moment she stared into the pair of green eyes that could only belong to a Steele.

"Well now, isn't that nice of Tyson Steele," Mo said with mock sweetness. "I wonder which one of us he wants to take home tonight."

"Take home?" Hunter asked, while her eyes remained on Tyson. For some reason she couldn't break her gaze. It was as if she was caught in the depths of those gorgeous green eyes.

"Yes, take home. He doesn't really date. He just has a history of one-night stands," Mo replied.

"Do we have to guess which one of us he's interested in?" Kat asked, chuckling, and then took a quick sip of her drink. "If you recall, Mo, that particular Steele was hot and heavy for Hunter back in the day."

"That's right. I remember." Mo turned to Hunter. "And if I recall, you dumped him. Probably the only female in this town with sense enough to do so."

With that reminder, Hunter tore her gaze from Tyson's to take a sip of her drink. In high school, Tyson, along with his five brothers, were known as the "Bad News" Steeles. Handsome as sin with green eyes they'd inherited from their mother, the six had a reputation as heartbreakers. It was widely known that their only interest in a girl was getting under her dress.

Galen Steele, the oldest of the bunch, had been a senior in high school when she'd been a freshman. Tyson was the second oldest. After Tyson came Eli, Jonas, Mercury and Gannon. Each brother was separated the closest in age by no more than eleven months, which meant their mother had practically been pregnant for six straight years.

"Tyson gave me no choice," Hunter said, finally replying to Mo's comment. "I liked him and for some reason I figured he would treat me differently since his family had been members of my grandfather's church. Boy, was I naive."

Kat chuckled. "But like Mo said, when you found

out that you'd be just another notch on his bedpost, at least you had the sense to dump him."

"I didn't dump him," Hunter said, sitting back in her chair. She didn't have to glance over at Tyson to know he was still staring at her. "When he told me what he wanted, I merely told him I saw no reason for us to continue to date, because he wasn't getting it."

"That's a dump," Mo said, grinning. "And be forewarned, nothing about the Steeles has changed. Those brothers are still bad news. Hard-core womanizers. Getting laid is still their favorite pastime."

"At least three had the sense to get married," Kat added, taking another sip of her drink.

"Oh? Which ones?" Hunter inquired.

"Galen, Eli and Jonas."

Hunter vaguely remembered Eli but she did remember Jonas since they'd graduated in the same class. And she couldn't help but recall Galen Steele. He had gotten expelled from school after the principal found him under the gymnasium bleachers making out with the man's daughter. His reputation around school was legendary. "So, Galen got married?"

"Yes, a few years ago, and his wife just gave birth to twins," Mo explained. "Last night, in fact. The announcement was in the papers this morning. It was a huge write-up in the society section."

Hunter nodded as she tried ignoring the fact Tyson still had his eyes on her. "What does Tyson do for a living?"

"He's a heart surgeon at Phoenix Baptist Hospital," Mo responded.

"Good for him. He always wanted to be a doctor."
She recalled their long talks, not knowing at the time
their conversations were just part of his plan to reel
her in. Unfortunately for him, she hadn't been biting.

"Don't look now, ladies, but Tyson has gotten up off
the bar stool and is headed this way."

Although Kat had told them not to look, Hunter
couldn't help doing so. She wished she hadn't when
Tyson's gaze captured hers. He'd been eye candy in his
teens and now eighteen years later he was doubly so.
She couldn't miss that air of arrogance that seemed to
surround him as he walked toward them. He appeared
so powerfully male that every step he took conveyed
primitive animal sexuality. There was no doubt in her
mind that over the years Tyson had sharpened his game
and was now an ace at getting whatever he wanted.

He was wearing a pair of dark slacks and a caramel-
colored pullover sweater. She was convinced that on any
other man the attire would look just so-so. But on Tyson,
the sweater emphasized his wide shoulders, and the
pants definitely did something to his masculine build.

"I understand whenever a Steele sees a woman he
wants, he goes after her. It appears Tyson's targeted
you, Hunter," Mo said as she leaned over. "Maybe he
thinks there's unfinished business between the two of
you. Eighteen years' worth."

Hunter waved off her friend's words. "Don't be silly.
He probably doesn't even remember me, it's been so
long."

It took less than a minute for Tyson to reach their
table. He glanced around and smiled at everyone. "Eve-

ning, ladies." And then his gaze returned to hers and
he said, "Hello, Hunter. It's been a while."

Hunter inhaled deeply, surprised that he *had* remembered her after all. But what really captured her attention were his features. He was still sinfully handsome,
with skin the color of creamy butternut and a mouth
that was shaped too darn beautifully to belong to any
man. And his voice was richer and a lot deeper than
she'd remembered.

Before she could respond to what he'd said, Mo and
Kat thanked him for the drinks as they stood. Hunter
looked at them. "Where are you two going?" she asked,
not missing the smirk on Mo's face.

"Kat and I thought we'd move closer to that big-
screen television to catch the last part of the basketball
game. I think my team is winning."

Hunter came close to calling Mo out by saying she
didn't have a team. She knew for a fact that neither Mo
nor Kat was into sports. Why were they deliberately
leaving her alone with Tyson?

As soon as they grabbed their drinks off the table
and walked away, Tyson didn't waste time claiming
one of the vacated seats. Hunter glanced over and met
his gaze while thinking that the only thing worse than
being deserted was being deserted and left with a Steele.

She took a sip of her drink and then said, "I want to
thank you for my drink, as well. That was nice of you."

"I'm a nice person."

The jury is still out on that, she thought. "I'm surprised you remember me, Tyson."

He chuckled, and the sound was so stimulating it

seemed to graze her skin. "Trust me. I remember you. And do you know what I remember most of all?"

"No, what?"

He leaned over the table as if to make sure his next words were for her ears only. "The fact that we never slept together."

Chapter 2

Tyson thought the shocked look on Hunter's face was priceless. He also thought it was a total turn-on. Up close she was even more beautiful. There had been something about her dark, almond-shaped eyes and long lashes that he'd always found alluring. But what was really getting to him was her lips, especially the bottom one. The curvy shape would entice any man to want to taste it. Nibble on it. Greedily devour it.

She interrupted his thoughts when she finally said, "And if you recall that, then I'm sure you remember why."

"Yes, I remember," he said, holding tight to her gaze. "You weren't one of those high school girls who slept around. You wanted me to make you my steady girlfriend and I had no intention of doing that."

"You just wanted me in the backseat of your car," she said.

He smiled. "The front seat would have worked just fine, trust me. I wanted you and my goal was to get you. For me it was all about sex then."

"Just like it's all about sex for you now?" she asked smoothly.

"Yes." He had no problem being up front with her or any woman, letting them know what he wanted, what he didn't want and, in her particular case, what he'd missed out on getting. She was the lone person in the "tried but failed" column. He intended to remedy that.

"I heard a while back that you'd gotten married, Hunter."

She took another sip of her drink and he remembered the one and only time he'd sampled the beautiful lips that kissed her glass. "Yes, I got married."

He looked down at her ringless hand before glancing back up at her. "Still married?"

"No."

Her response was quick and biting, which only led him to believe the divorce had been unpleasant. That might be bad news for her, but he saw it as good news for him since he was known to inject new life into divorcées. Over the years he'd taken plenty to bed, not necessarily to mend their broken hearts, but mainly to prove there was life after a shitty marriage.

"How long ago?"

Her eyebrows lifted. "Why do you want to know?"

"Just curious."

For a second, she didn't respond, and then she said, "Two years."

He nodded as he leaned back in his chair. "Sorry to hear about your divorce," he said, although he was anything but. Although his parents had a great marriage and it seemed his three brothers' marriages were off to a good start, he was of the opinion that marriage wasn't for everybody. It definitely wasn't for him and evidently hadn't been for her.

"No need to be sorry, Tyson. I regret the day I ever married the bastard."

He'd heard that line before. And as far as he was concerned there was no need for her to expound. It really didn't matter to him what she thought of her ex. What mattered was that divorcées were his specialty. He would gladly shift her from his "tried and failed" column to his "achieved" category. Every one of his senses was focused on getting her into his bed.

"So what brings you back to Phoenix, Hunter?" he asked with a smile.

Hunter was glad a waiter appeared at that moment to place a drink in front of Tyson. Evidently he was a regular, since the man had known just what to give him. It took only a minute but that had been enough time to get herself together and recover from Tyson's charismatic personality. It was quite obvious that he was a man on the prowl tonight and had set his sights on her. Mo and Kat had said as much, but at the time she hadn't believed them. The man had been a player in high school and eighteen years later he was still at it. She couldn't help wondering why he hadn't gotten past that mentality.

"Now, where were we? Oh, yes. I asked what brings you back to Phoenix."

She took another sip of her drink. There was no way she would tell him how after their divorce and the dissolution of their partnership, her architect husband had underhandedly taken all their clients. Starting over in Boston would not have been so bad if he hadn't deliberately tried to sabotage her reputation as an architect. Tyson didn't have to know that because of her husband's actions she'd decided to start over here. Instead of telling him all of that, she decided to tell him the other reason she'd come back home.

"My parents."

He lifted a brow. "Are they ill?"

She shook her head. "No, they aren't ill. My brother thinks they're having too much fun."

Hunter realized just how ridiculous that sounded and added, "A few months ago they purchased 'his and hers' Harleys, and before that they signed up to take sky-diving lessons. Lately, they've been hinting at selling the house and buying a boat to sail around the world."

Tyson appeared amused. "Sounds to me like they're enjoying life. Maybe your brother needs to take a chill pill."

"Possibly, but his hands are full right now with his teenage sons and he feels Mom and Dad are driving him as crazy as they claim he's driving them. I decided it was best I came home to keep peace." Hunter had no idea how she would manage to do that. Her parents were intent on having fun and her brother was intent on getting them to act their age.

"You're an architect, right?" he asked her.

"Yes. How did you know?"

"Someone mentioned it at one of the class reunions that you never attended."

He was right, she hadn't attended any. At first it had been school keeping her away, and later trying to build her career and finally trying to save her marriage. Although Carter had made sure they attended all of his high school reunions, he had been dead set against attending any of hers, and as usual she'd given in to him.

"I understand you're a doctor."

He nodded. "Yes. A heart surgeon."

She smiled. "And I bet you're a good one."

"I owe it to my patients to do my very best."

And there was no doubt in Hunter's mind that he did. She remembered he was devoted to whatever he did, even if he was chasing girls.

"I'm glad you're back in Phoenix, Hunter."

"Why?" She really couldn't understand why he would be.

He leaned in closer. "Because we have history."

She couldn't keep the smile from tugging at her lips. "History?"

"Yes."

"What kind of history?"

"I think of you as the one who got away."

She had to keep from laughing out loud at that. "You mean the one who never made it to the backseat of your car?"

"Pretty much."

"It's been eighteen years. I would think you'd have gotten over it by now."

He shook his head and chuckled. "I had. However, seeing you again brought it back home to me, so I've come up with a plan."

She lifted a brow. "What kind of plan?"

"A plan to seduce you."

Hunter's breath caught in her lungs. His audacity was almost as great as his arrogance. What man told a woman he planned to seduce her? "Seriously? Do you think it will be that easy?"

The smile that appeared on his face almost made her heart miss a beat. Although all the Steele brothers had those killer green eyes, she recalled that Tyson and Mercury were the only ones with dimples. Why was it that whenever he flashed those dimples, her pulse rate went haywire?

"I didn't say it would be easy," he said smoothly. "What I said was that i had a plan. i see no reason that we can't rekindle what we had years ago."

"There's nothing to rekindle. Need I remind you that we didn't have anything mainly because you were only interested in one thing?"

His smile widened as he lifted his drink to his lips. Without saying a word, he was letting her know that nothing about him had changed and that he was still only interested in one thing.

"I suggest you go find someone else to seduce."

He shook his head. "I can't do that. I want you."

"You can't always have what you want. That's life."

Whatever he was about to say was lost when Mo and Kat appeared. "My team lost," Mo said, grinning. She glanced at her watch. "Tomorrow is a workday so we figured it's time to go."

Great timing, Hunter thought, and she stood.

Tyson stood as well and shoved his hands into his pockets. "I'll take you home, Hunter, if you aren't ready to leave just yet."

If he thought for one minute she would go with him, especially after admitting his plan to seduce her, he wasn't thinking straight. "Thanks, but I am ready. It was good seeing you again, Tyson."

"Same here, Hunter," he said, and she thought she saw something akin to amusement in his eyes. "I have a feeling we'll be running into each other again."

Hunter hoped not. She had enough to worry about with her parents, without being concerned about Tyson Steele trying to get her into bed. "Good night." She walked toward the door with Mo and Kat, feeling the heat of Tyson's gaze on her backside.

As soon as they were out the door she turned to her friends. "Why on earth did the two of you leave me alone with Tyson?"

Kat grinned. "Because we knew you could handle him."

"Besides, it was quite obvious you were the one on his radar and not us," Mo added. "So how did it go?"

Hunter shook her head. "You guys were right. Nothing has changed with Tyson. He's still looking for a pair of legs to get between."

"And you didn't make yours available to him again?" Kat asked, grinning. "What a shame."

"For him I'm sure it was, especially since he told me of his plan to seduce me."

Mo's eyes widened. "He actually told you that?"

"Without cracking a smile or blinking an eye."

Both Mo and Kat stopped walking to stare at her. "You don't sound worried."

Hunter stopped and glanced at her friends, lifting a brow. "Why would I be?"

"We're talking about Tyson Steele, Hunter. The man who's known to get what he wants. I heard from women that he's so smooth you won't miss your panties until they're gone. And for him to already have a plan of seduction for you sounds serious."

"Only in his book, not mine."

Kat tilted her head. "And this from a woman who's gone without sex for two years now."

"Actually four. If you recall, Carter and I slept in separate bedrooms for two years before our divorce. You can't miss what you never got on a regular basis anyway. I haven't had an orgasm in so long I've honestly forgotten how it feels."

"Then you're in luck," Mo said with a huge smile on her face. "There are quite a few women around town who claim the orgasms those Bad News Steeles give a girl can blow her mind to smithereens and have her begging for more. Rumor has it that you haven't truly been made love to unless it's been by a Steele. They're supposed to be just that good in the bedroom."

Hunter rolled her eyes. "I'm sure it's nothing more than a lot of hype."

"But what if it's not?" Kat asked seriously. "And just think. One of those Bad News Steeles has plans to seduce you. If Tyson succeeds then you'll never forget how an orgasm feels again."

"Whatever," Hunter said as they resumed walking. By the time they reached the car, Hunter decided whatever plan Tyson thought he had for her was no big deal, since she doubted their paths would cross again anyway. And even if they did, she was certain it was just like she'd told Mo and Kat. All those rumors about the Steeles were probably nothing more than a lot of hype.

"Is there a reason you're visiting me this time of night, Tyson?" Eli Steele asked gruffly, moving aside for his brother to enter his home. "And why aren't you at the basketball game with Mercury and Gannon?"

"I had better things to do."

Eli rolled his eyes. "In other words, your team didn't make it to the finals. Everyone knows what a sore loser you are."

Tyson frowned. "I'm not a sore loser." He then glanced around. "Where's Stacey?"

His once die-hard bachelor brother had defected and married, just like his brothers Galen and Jonas. The only thing redeeming about that was he'd married Stacey Carlson. She was the sister of a good friend and former colleague of Tyson's by the name of Cohen.

"Stacey's in bed, where most people with good sense are by now," Eli said, dropping down on the sofa. "I hear Brittany and the babies might be going home tomorrow."

Tyson nodded. "So I heard."

"Word also has it that Mom has volunteered to help out for a few days. I hope she doesn't get on Galen's nerves."

Tyson chuckled. "I doubt that she will. He's been in her good graces ever since he was the first to get married. Besides, helping out with the babies will keep her busy."

"And the busier she is the less chance she has to get into your business—and Mercury's and Gannon's—right?"

"Right," Tyson said, knowing Eli understood. Before he married, he'd gotten the Eden Tyson Steele's "sticking her nose where it doesn't belong" treatment, just like the rest of them. Now, with three sons married, she was relentless on the other three, prodding them along to get them to the altar. Tyson vowed it wouldn't work on him. "So who do you think the babies look like?"

Eli chuckled. "With those green eyes, forehead and lips, they favor Galen all the way. I haven't heard their decisions on names, have you?"

"Nope, but rumor has it they're allowing Mom to do the honors."

Eli shook his head. "No wonder she's blowing up the newspapers. She's up there on cloud nine."

"Fine. She can stay there for a while," Tyson said. "Just as long as she's not into my business while she's up there."

"You and Mercury and Gannon will get a slight reprieve, but don't think she'll let you guys off the hook for good." Eli didn't say anything for a minute as he stared across the room at his brother and then he said, "Okay, get it out. There's a reason you dropped by so late."

Tyson sat down in the wingback chair across from the sofa. "There is. Hunter McKay's back in town."

Eli's forehead bunched. "Who's Hunter McKay?"

Tyson rolled his eyes. "I can't believe you don't remember Hunter. But I shouldn't be surprised. Back in the day, the old Eli remembered bodies and not names."

A smile curved Eli's lips. "True. So was she one of those bodies?"

"Hell, no! She was my girl."

"You never had a girl, Tyson."

His brother was right and for the life of him Tyson wasn't sure why he'd said what he had just now. "Sorry, saying that was a huge mistake."

"I hope there's not a reason why you made it. And lower your voice or you'll wake up my wife and she needs her rest."

Tyson didn't need to ask why. It seemed that all his married brothers had wedded women they enjoyed spending time with in and out of the bedroom. "There's not a reason."

Eli stared at him for a long moment and then asked, "So what's the big deal about this Hunter McKay being back in town?"

"It just is."

"Hey, wait a minute," Eli said, sitting straight up on the sofa. "That name is coming back to me. Isn't Hunter

McKay the girl who dumped you in your senior year of high school?"

"She didn't dump me."

"That's not the way I remember it. And why are you interested in Hunter McKay? Didn't I hear something about her getting married some years back?"

"She's a divorcée now. I saw her tonight at Notorious and got that much out of her. And it was a nasty divorce."

"How do you know?"

Tyson stretched his long legs out in front of him. "She called her ex a bastard."

"Okay, her ex was a bastard. That doesn't explain why you're here at midnight."

Without hesitation Tyson said, "I want you to find out information on her."

Eli rolled his eyes. "Do I look like a friggin' detective?"

"No, but she's an architect and as president of Phoenix's business council, you would know if she's set up her own business in town or was hired by an established firm."

"And you want to know that for what reason?"

Tyson's lips curved into a smile. "Because I plan to seduce her. And before you conveniently forget your own reputation before marrying Stacey and start acting holier-than-thou, just for your information, I gave Hunter McKay fair warning of my intentions tonight."

"You actually told her that you plan to seduce her?"

"Yes. You know how I operate, Eli. I don't play games and divorcées are my specialty. I'll be doing her a favor, especially if her ex was the bastard she claims he was."

Eli frowned. "You claim you gave her fair warning, so now I'm going to give you the same, Tyson. I had a plan for Stacey, although my plan was different from yours. My plan backfired. In my case it was for the best. My advice to you is to tread lightly and with caution, or you're liable to get possessed by passion. Once that happens, it will be all over for you."

Tyson frowned. "Possessed by passion? What the hell are you talking about?"

"You're cocky enough to think that once you get Hunter McKay in your bed, you're going to blow her mind."

Tyson smiled confidently. "Of course."

"Have you given any thought to the possibility that she'll end up blowing yours?"

Tyson stared hard at his brother. "No, I haven't given it any thought because *that* won't be happening."

Chapter 3

Hunter studied the older woman sitting across her desk. Pauline Martin had come to her highly recommended by Hunter's brother, Bernie, who was a good friend of the woman's son. Ms. Martin's husband had died last year and she wanted to do something other than stay in the house and stare at the walls. The administrative assistant position seemed perfect for her. From the interview, Hunter had known she was just what McKay Architecture Firm needed. Now if she could only get some clients.

She was scheduled to meet with an advertising firm later that day to discuss ideas on how she could promote her business. There were a number of architectural companies in Phoenix and the key to succeeding was to make sure hers stood out.

Hunter stood. "I'm looking forward to us working together, Pauline, and I'll see you in the morning."

"Thanks, Hunter."

An hour or so later Hunter had snapped her briefcase closed to leave for the day. Starting over in a business wasn't easy but, as her parents had reminded her that morning when she'd stopped by their house for breakfast, she was a fighter. What Carter had done was wrong, but instead of getting bitter, she had to do better. She had to look ahead and not look back. No matter what, she couldn't let him break her.

And more than anything, she couldn't believe all men were like Carter Robinson. Had he really expected her to remain his wife while he engaged in all those affairs? And when she had confronted him about it, he'd only laughed and told her to get over it. He'd said she wouldn't leave him because she had too much to lose, and that no matter what she accused him of, his family would stick by his side.

And they had.

Even his mother, who'd said she sympathized with Hunter over her son's wretched behavior, had stuck by him in the end. For Hunter, that had hurt more than anything because she'd assumed she and Nadine Robinson had had a good and close relationship. At least they had until the day Hunter had decided to bring her eight-year marriage to Carter to an end. Then Nadine had proven Carter right. Blood had been thicker than water.

Even with Carter's high-priced divorce lawyer, at least the judge who'd handled the divorce had sided with her and ordered Carter to give her fifty percent equity out of the company. He hadn't even wanted to do that. And the judge had been more than fair in making sure he did the same with their home, as well as all the other assets Carter had acquired over the years. Some she hadn't known about until the day the private investigator she'd hired had uncovered them.

So now she was back in Phoenix. In a way she felt like a stranger in her own hometown, since she'd made Boston her home ever since enrolling in MIT for her graduate degree. She'd been working a few years when she'd met Carter at a fund-raiser her architecture firm had given. He was a member of the Boston Robinsons, a family that took pride in their old-money status and the rich history that came with it.

They'd been married three years when she'd first found about Carter's affairs. He swore they meant nothing and begged her to forgive him, and she had. He became attentive for a year or two, and they'd even tried having a family, but with no success. Hunter wasn't exactly sure when his affairs had picked back up again, but she'd begun noticing the usual—lipstick on the collar, the scent of another woman's perfume and suspicious text messages. That's when she hired a private investigator. The PI's report had been the last straw. There was no way she could remain married to Carter after that, regardless of what her in-laws thought. In the end, they had sided with Carter in his campaign to destroy her.

She drew in a deep breath, refusing to give in to her sorrows. Somewhere out there were women in far worse situations than she. Her grandmother used to repeat that adage about making lemons into lemonade and Hunter intended to do just that.

At that moment the image of Tyson Steele came into her mind. Not that it had actually ever left since they'd run into each other last night. In fact she had dreamed about him. Of all things, in her dream she had let him do what she had refused to let him do eighteen years ago, and that was to take her in the backseat of a car.

Hunter shook her head. She couldn't believe how scandalous that dream had been and it was even worse that she had totally and thoroughly enjoyed it. Luckily it had been just a dream and not the real thing. But the dream had been enough. She had awakened panting, with heated lust rushing through every part of her. It had taken a long cold shower to calm down her body.

During the four years of her sexless life, the last thing she had thought about was having an affair. So why now? And why Tyson Steele? He was arrogant, confident and too cocky to suit her. They hadn't held a conversation for more than a few minutes before he was telling her of his plans to seduce her.

She shook her head as she headed for the door. Some men's attitudes simply amazed her. But then again, he was a Steele. Hearing three of his brothers had married meant there could be hope for him, but she wouldn't be crazy enough to put any money on that assumption.

But what really should be hilarious was that Tyson Steele thought he could seduce her. She figured he'd been all talk and that his words had been meant to get her sexually riled up, and they had…to a point. After her shower this morning her common sense was firmly back in place. All it had taken was a look around her apartment to remember all she'd lost because of a man. The last thing she needed was to get involved with another man for any reason.

But what about just for sex?

She almost missed her step when the idea popped in her head. Where had such a thought come from? She was a good girl. The granddaughter of a retired minister. A woman who'd always worked hard, played fair and been a good wife to her husband. And as Nadine had often claimed, the best daughter-in-law anyone could ask for.

Yet, regardless of all those things, she'd gotten royally screwed. And because of all those things Carter had figured she would never leave him. That she would stay married to him regardless. What he'd failed to take into consideration was that everyone had a breaking point. When she had taken as much as she could, she had walked away without looking back. She only wished she'd been strong enough to do it sooner.

As she locked up her office she figured she might as well dream about Tyson Steele again tonight. Dreams were safe. Besides, she had no reason to think their paths would cross again. For one, she didn't intend to return to that nightclub where he apparently hung out.

His parents attended the same church as hers, the one where her grandfather had been pastor before he'd passed away years ago. During breakfast this morning she'd deliberately asked her mother to bring her up-to-date on church members, former and present. It seemed the Steeles were still members of their church, and her mother said that although she would see Eden and Drew Steele on most Sundays, she rarely saw their sons and couldn't recall the last time one of them attended church.

Deciding she didn't want to think about Tyson Steele, she stepped inside the elevator to leave the office.

Tyson had stepped out of the shower and was toweling off when his cell phone rang. He recognized the ring tone. It was Eli. With three surgeries today back to back, he hadn't time to think about much of anything but his patients. The surgeries had gone well and he'd delivered good news to the families. Before leaving the hospital, he had made his rounds, completed his reports and given final instructions to the nurses caring for his patients. Now he was at home, on full alert and eager for any information his brother had for him.

He grabbed the phone off the vanity. "Eli, did you find out anything?"

"This is going to cost you."

Tyson rolled his eyes. "Who do you think I am? Galen?"

It was a running joke in the family that Galen worked the least but made the most. While attending college Galen and his two roommates had decided to do something to make money and since all three were computer-savvy, they created video games. After their games became a hit on campus, they formed a business and by the time they graduated from college they were millionaires. The three were still partners today and usually released one game a year around the holiday season. Galen enjoyed flaunting the fact that he was able to work less than twenty hours a week and still make millions.

Eli chuckled. "With twins Galen won't have as much free time on his hands."

Tyson smiled at the thought. "You think?"

"We can hope."

Tyson tossed the towel aside to slide into a pair of briefs. "So what did you find out about Hunter McKay? Did she establish a company here?"

"Yes. She opened an architect office in the Double-Row building a week ago." Eli paused a minute and then said, "And you were right. Her divorce from her husband was pretty nasty."

"How do you know?"

"The one good thing about being president of the business council of a major city is getting to meet other such individuals. The one from Boston, John Wrigley, and I have become pretty good friends. I gave John a call today. According to him, Hunter divorced her husband on grounds of adultery and had the goods from a PI to prove it. Her ex hired this high-priced attorney to fight to keep Hunter from getting a fifty-fifty split of the architectural firm they owned together, but the judge sided with Hunter. In the end Hunter's ex retaliated by making sure she didn't get any of their clients."

The man was a bastard just like Hunter McKay said, Tyson thought, easing a T-shirt over his head. "I think I'll pay her a visit tomorrow."

"That doesn't surprise me."

"As a client," Tyson added.

"A client? That *does* surprise me. I didn't know you were interested in getting a house designed."

Tyson smiled. "I wasn't before now."

"Hell, Tyson, you don't even own any land."

Tyson's smile widened. "Shouldn't be that hard to buy some." Even through the phone line Tyson could imagine Eli rolling his eyes.

"And you would go to all that trouble just for a woman?"

Tyson thought about his brother's question. "But she's not just any woman. She's the one who got away. And now she's back."

The next morning Hunter walked into her office and stopped dead in her tracks. Her eyes did a double take. Was Tyson Steele actually sitting in her reception area, chatting so amiably with Pauline that neither noticed her entry?

"Good morning," she said, breaking into their conversation.

Pauline and Tyson both glanced up, and Pauline smiled brightly. Tyson stood as he gave her a slow perusal, his gaze moving over her from head to toe. His eyes returned to meet hers and she tried ignoring the acceleration of her heart, a result of the intensity of his stare.

What were the odds that the same man she had been dreaming about for the past two nights would be in her office this morning? And they were the kind of dreams that heated her just by remembering them.

An excited Pauline interrupted her thoughts. "Good morning, Hunter. I think we might have our first client."

"Do we?" Hunter asked, her gaze switching from Tyson to Pauline.

"Yes. Dr. Tyson Steele is here to see you about designing his home."

Hunter found that hard to believe, especially after what he'd told her two nights ago. He was more interested in seducing her than anything else. "Is he?"

"Yes, I am," Tyson said.

She tried ignoring the slow, languorous heat that flowed through her body at the sound of Tyson's deep, husky voice. She looked back over at him and wished she hadn't. She'd thought he was sinfully handsome when she'd seen him at the nightclub, but as he stood in the sunlight streaming through her office window he looked triply so. The man was totally gorgeous, one hundred percent male perfection. He looked like scrumptious eye candy in his jeans and dark gray hooded sweatshirt. For her, there was just something about a nice male body in a pair of jeans and it was almost too much for her this early in the morning.

"In that case, Dr. Steele, you and I definitely need to talk," she said, moving toward her office.

She heard Tyson close her office door behind him the moment she set her briefcase on her desk. She turned around and fought back the urge to moan. The way he was leaning back against the closed door, he was sexiness personified. And his razor-sharp green eyes were on her. Why, today of all days, had she worn a dress, one shorter than she would normally wear? Shorter but still

appropriate for conducting business. Yet from the way
Tyson was staring at her, one would think otherwise.
In fact, one would think she didn't have on any clothes
at all. Sexual vibes were pouring off him in droves and
she could feel desire flowing through her veins.

Clearing her throat as she tried getting control of the
situation, she said, "Please have a seat, Tyson, and tell
me just what it is that you want."

Realizing that wasn't a good question to ask him,
she rephrased it. "Tell me what design of home you're
interested in."

Tyson thought she had asked the right question the
first time. He certainly had no problem telling her exactly what he wanted. But first he had to get his libido
back in check. It had begun smoldering big-time when
he'd glanced up from his conversation with her administrative assistant to see her standing there. She was
what sexual fantasies were made of, and when it came
to her he had plenty.

She was a constant visitor to his nightly dreams. If
that wasn't bad enough she'd also crept into his day-
time thoughts. All this from a woman he hadn't seen in
years. Usually he didn't waste time fantasizing about
any one woman before moving quickly to another. But
it seemed he was focused on Hunter McKay and no one
else, and he couldn't figure out why.

Eli thought he was obsessed with her and Tyson was
beginning to wonder if that was true. He had never been
obsessed with a woman before and was convinced he
only wanted her in his bed, nothing more. Every time

he thought about them having sex his pulse went crazy. He couldn't help wondering if there was more to his desire for Hunter than her being the one who got away. Why was he turned on by almost everything about her? Like her dress, for instance.

He knew it was just a dress, but on her it looked simply fantastic. He especially liked the way it complemented her legs. The other night she'd been wearing slacks so today was the first time he'd seen them. Now it came back to him that in high school, she had been a majorette, and the one thing he had liked was that she had a gorgeous pair of legs. She still did. And in that dress and a pair of three-inch pumps, she was definitely presenting challenges to his peace of mind. She looked neat, professional and way too appealing.

"Tyson?"

Hunter's voice brought his focus back to their conversation. He stepped away from the door and slid into a chair across from her desk. Doing so put him in close proximity to her and he enjoyed inhaling her scent. She was wearing the same perfume she had the other night and he thought the fragrance was definitely her signature. He met her eyes and said, "I have no problem telling you what I want." He let that statement hang in the air between them for a moment before adding, "As far as a design for a house, of course."

"Of course," Hunter said, moving around her desk to sit down behind it. "Before I can help you there are a few things I would need to know," she said, picking up a notepad and pen.

"Like what?"

"Like the location of the property the house will be built on. I need to verify there aren't any restrictions in the area that might prevent you from building the type of home you want. And I need to make sure your lot is large enough to fit whatever design you have in mind."

He nodded. "I find your inquiries interesting. Why don't we have dinner tonight and talk about them?"

She leaned back in her chair and stared at him. "We need to discuss it now, Tyson, because I have no intentions of having dinner with you."

"Why?"

"Because after work is my time. A business dinner means extending my work time into my pleasure time."

"We can make it both."

Her mouth flattened into a hard line. "No, we can't, and I don't have time to play games. If the only reason for your visit is to—"

"Try my hand at seducing you?"

She held his stare. "You warned me the other night that would be your main objective."

A soft chuckle escaped his lips. "It still is. Trust me. I haven't changed my mind about it. But I do want to talk about a house design, as well."

Tyson was serious about that. Although he would admit he'd initially had an ulterior motive for seeking her out today, all it had taken was for him to wake up to the noise outside his window to know he had put off moving long enough. Currently, he leased a condo in a very prestigious area of Phoenix not far from the hospital. It was large and spacious and had a great view of the mountains. But unfortunately it came with some drawbacks. Like the close proximity of his neighbors. Over the years he had gotten used to car doors slamming, horns honking and the early morning ruckus of parents hustling their kids off to school. Maybe it was time to pursue his dream of living in the countryside.

She was still staring at him, as if she was trying to figure out if he really was serious about getting a house designed. He decided to put her mind at ease. "What you might see as a problem is the fact that I haven't purchased the property yet. It doesn't matter, Hunter. You design my house and when I get ready to build it I'll buy enough land for it to sit on."

She was still staring and he had no problem with her doing so because he knew she was also thinking about him. Sizing him up. Trying to figure him out. He wished he could tell her not to bother because he was too complex for her to try.

"I need to ask you something, Tyson," she finally said after a few moments had passed.

"Yes?"

"When did you decide you wanted a house designed, and why did you come to me?"

He could tell her about his conversation with Eli yesterday, but decided to omit that part. "To be honest with you, I hadn't given much thought of designing a house. I live in a condo and that suited me just fine. However, I knew you were an architect and I knew my plans for you, so I decided I wanted to see your work."

"Let me get this straight," she said, sitting up in her chair. "You planned to seduce me so you came up with the idea to have me design a home for you. A home you never thought about owning until after you saw me the other night. You would go to all that trouble to get a woman in your bed?"

He couldn't help the smile that curved his lips. "No. I wouldn't go to all that trouble to get a woman in my bed, Hunter. But I would go to all that trouble to get you there."

She frowned. "Don't waste your time."

"It won't be. I know women, Hunter. I can read them as well as any book that's ever been published. You gave me the same looks I was giving you at Notorious. The 'I want to sleep with you' looks."

"I was not!"

"Yes, you were. Maybe you didn't realize you were doing so, but you were. The sexual chemistry between us was strong that night. I felt it and I saw no need to play games. That's why I told you my intentions up front. Did you honestly expect me not to explore all those heated vibes you and I were giving off that night?"

"But to invent this—"

"I didn't invent anything. What I've done is take another look at my living situation. Of my brothers I'm the only one who doesn't own a home. Never gave much thought to doing so. My condo is not far from the hospital and pretty convenient to everything I want. But this morning I noticed things I had chosen to ignore. Like the closeness of my neighbors. The noise and such. And the more I thought about it, the more that house in the country, the one I had thought about building years ago when I first got out of med school, suddenly appealed to me again. So I thought—"

"That since I was an architect and you had plans to seduce me anyway, that you would kill two birds with one stone?"

"I guess that's one way to look at it."

Hunter shook her head. After a minute she said, "That night after I left the club I thought about you a lot."

"You did?"

She heard the delight in his voice. "Yes, I did. I tried convincing myself that I imagined it. There was no way that at after eighteen years you were as arrogant and conceited as you were back in high school. But, Tyson, I was wrong. You are. You assume all you have to do is say what you want and you'll get it. You love women, although you'll never fall *in* love with one. You enjoy sharing your bed with them but that's about all you'll ever share. You—"

"Don't blame me," he interrupted. "Blame my father."

She lifted a brow. "Your father? What does your father have to do with it?"

Tyson smiled. "I'm Drew Steele's son. My brothers and I inherited his genes. We got some from Mom, of course, but the womanizing ones came from my dad. He used to be a player of the worst kind in his day, and even got run out of Charlotte because of his scandalous ways."

"And you're actually using your father's past behavior as an excuse for yours?"

"Like I said, it's in the genes. But since my father

is happily married to my mother and has been for over thirty years, I figure there's hope for me and my brothers. At least my mother is convinced there is and she might be right. Three have gotten married within a three-year period. Not that I have any interest in getting married, now or ever."

"I don't blame you," she said, not able to stop herself. "I tried it once and once was enough." He would never know just how much she meant those words.

"Are you going through the 'I hate all men' stage?"

She tried not to notice the breadth of his shoulders when he leaned back in his chair. Or the way his jeans stretched tight over his muscular thighs. "I have no reason to hate all men, Tyson. In truth, I don't hate my ex. I pity him."

He held her gaze. "So the reason you won't share my bed has nothing to do with him."

"No. It's mainly because of your attitude."

"My attitude?"

"Yes."

"What's wrong with my attitude?"

"You act entitled."

"Do I?"

"Yes. I guess it's from women always letting you have your way. Giving you whatever you want. They make it too easy for you."

"And you intend to make things difficult, Hunter?"

A smile touched her lips. "I intend to make things impossible, Tyson."

"Nothing is impossible."

He stood and she couldn't help but admire how sexily

his body eased out of the chair. "And since you won't have dinner with me, how about lunch tomorrow?"

"Give me one good reason why I should."

"Because I'm a potential client who merely wants to discuss ideas about the kind of country home I want you to design for me."

Hunter stared at him. Was he really serious about wanting her to design his home? There was only one way to find out. "Lunch tomorrow will be fine. Make an appointment with Pauline on your way out."

"No, I'm making one with you now. Put me on your calendar for tomorrow. Noon. At Gabriel's. I'll meet you there."

He headed for the door. When he reached it, he turned around and smiled. "And you look good today, by the way. Good enough to eat."

And then he opened the door and left.

Chapter 4

Hunter was convinced she should have her head examined when she arrived at Gabriel's the next day at noon. Meeting Tyson for lunch wasn't a smart move. So why was she here? Even if Tyson wanted her to design his country home there were ulterior motives behind it. He had been up front about his plans for her. It was all about seduction. Plain and simple. But he would discover there wasn't anything plain or simple about it.

The last thing she needed was to get mixed up with Tyson, or any man for that matter. She had put her divorce behind her, moved to be closer to her family and start over in her business. Hard work lay ahead of her and she had very little time to indulge in an affair. Besides, hadn't a failed eight-year marriage proved she was lousy at relationships?

"May I help you, madam?"

"Yes," she said, glancing around. "I'm meeting Tyson Steele for lunch."

The maître d' smiled. "Yes. Dr. Steele arrived a few moments ago and requested one of our private rooms in the back. I'll lead the way."

"Thanks," she said, following behind the man. A private room? In the back? She didn't like the sound of that and had a mind to turn around and walk out. But Tyson was a client. And so far, he was the only one she had. She kept telling herself that once the advertisements she'd approved finally ran, business would pick up. She certainly hoped so.

The maître d' opened the door then stepped aside for her to enter. She looked around and saw Tyson. He stood and she could feel the air between them sizzle. She knew he felt it as well when she saw heat smoldering in the depths of his green eyes.

He must have come straight from the hospital since he was still wearing his physician jacket. Tightening her hand on her briefcase, she moved forward and tried to fight the attraction she felt toward him. "Tyson."

"Hunter. Glad you could join me." As if only realizing his attire, he took off his white coat. "Sorry, an emergency detained me."

No need to say she hoped it wasn't anything serious, because he was a heart surgeon, so anything he did was serious. "No problem. I know your time is valuable so we can go ahead and—"

"You look good again today."

"Thanks." Knowing they would be meeting for

lunch, she had worn a pantsuit. The way he had checked out her legs yesterday had been too unnerving. "As I said yesterday, usually a client has purchased property, but since—"

"We'll discuss business later. Let's order first. I'm starving. I've been in surgery all morning and missed breakfast."

"Oh. Of course." She glanced down at the menu and tried ignoring the tingles of awareness going through her. It wasn't easy sitting across the table from such a sexy man. So far he seemed all business and hadn't said anything she considered inappropriate. She wouldn't hold that compliment on how she looked against him. In fact she appreciated him making the observation. Carter had stopped telling her how good she looked even when she'd gone out of her way to please him.

"I already know what I want."

She glanced up and swallowed deeply at the look she saw in his eyes. She wasn't imagining the sizzling undercurrents flowing between them. "Do you?"

"Yes."

She held his gaze and the sexual tension surrounding them began mounting. He had been referring to what he wanted off the menu, hadn't he? With Tyson, one could never be sure. She'd discovered that often his words had a double meaning. "That was fast," she said, breaking his gaze to look back down at her menu.

"I've never been accused of being slow, Hunter."

She glanced back up at him again. "And what did you decide to get?"

"The pork chops. That's what I usually get whenever I come here."

She nodded. He had been talking about what was on the menu, after all. "The pork chops sound good."

"They are and that's what I want for now. What I really want I'll put on the back burner until…"

She glanced up to find his focus totally on her, making the undercurrents between them sizzle even more. "Until what?"

"I can bring you around to my way of thinking."

Hunter couldn't help but chuckle.

"And what do you find amusing, Hunter?"

She leaned forward in her chair. "For a minute there I thought this would be one of those rare times that you would be good."

"I am good. Always."

His words flowed through her and with supreme effort she tried not to imagine just how good he would be. "I was referring to your behavior."

"Now, *that*, not always. According to my mother I can push the envelope at times."

She bet. Hunter was glad the waiter returned and with the amount of food Tyson ordered it was apparent he hadn't lied about being hungry. She wondered where he would put it all.

As if reading her thoughts, he said, "I plan to work it off later."

"I don't doubt that you will."

He reached across the table and his fingers caressed her hand. "I don't mean with another woman, Hunter. I have a membership at the gym."

She wondered what had given away her thoughts and figured it must have been her tone. Why had the thought of him sleeping with a woman bothered her? And why did him caressing her hand send shivers of desire through her? "You don't owe me an explanation. What you do and with whom is your business, Tyson. And need I remind you," she said, pulling her hand back, "that this is a business meeting?"

"Duly reminded," he said, smiling. "Temptation got the best of me."

Although she wouldn't admit to it, temptation had almost gotten the best of her, as well. She had loved the feel of his touch and could still feel the imprint of his hand on her skin. It was becoming pretty clear that this attraction between her and Tyson could lead to big trouble if she wasn't careful. Deciding to break up the sexual tension flowing between them, she steered the conversation to an innocuous topic. "So how are your niece and nephew?"

He lifted a brow. "I take it you read that article in the paper, as well."

She shook her head. "No, Mo did and mentioned it the other night."

He took a sip of his water before answering. "Brittany and the twins are home now. I got a chance to see them before they left the hospital yesterday and they're doing fine. Galen is doing okay, too. In fact, he's on cloud nine."

"I can't picture him married."

"I couldn't, either, but it happened. And I'll admit

there's something pretty special between him and Brittany."

"She's not from here, right?"

"No. She's from Florida. She was in town on business when they met."

"Have they named the twins yet?"

"They gave my mother the honor and she came up with Ethan and Elyse."

A smile spread across Hunter's lips. "Oh, I like that."

"My brothers and I figured she couldn't help but seize the opportunity to give the twins names starting with the letter E to match hers."

Then he smiled and Hunter was amazed he could be even more handsome. But he was.

As they ate, Tyson tried not to glance over at Hunter. Conversation between them had stopped, and he couldn't help wondering what she was thinking. Although whatever thoughts going through her head were a mystery to him, those going through his own head were not. Simply put, he wanted her. How could a woman he hadn't seen in eighteen years hold his interest like she was doing? It didn't make sense. No woman had ever gotten to him this way and without any effort on her part. At least not any conscious effort. He doubted she was aware of just how alluring she was without even trying.

Even wearing a pantsuit he didn't miss her small waist and sexy curves. And on more than one occasion when he'd glanced at her while they were eating, he hadn't missed the hardened tips of her nipples beneath her blue silk shirt. That meant she wasn't as immune to him as she pretended to be. And when he had reached out to stroke her hand, he'd felt the sparks and knew she had, as well.

Somehow Hunter had managed to eradicate thoughts of other women from his mind. He hadn't even bothered dropping by Notorious last night. Instead, he had gone to his brother Jonas's house and stayed for dinner. Jonas's wife, Nikki, was an excellent cook and spoiled Jonas with all her delicious meals. Luckily neither Jonas nor Nikki seemed to mind his drop-in dinner visits.

He glanced over at Hunter again and liked the way she worked her mouth while chewing her food. He felt a tightening in his gut at the thought of her working that same mouth on him. And although his pork chop tasted good, as usual, he had a feeling she would taste even better. He closed his eyes and in his mind he could taste her. As sweet as honey.

"It's *that* good?"

He popped his eyes back open. "What?"

"Your pork chop. You had your eyes closed as if savoring the taste."

He wondered what her reaction would be if he confessed that he'd been thinking about her and not the pork chop. "Yes, it is good. Moist. Tender. Just the way I like it. What about your meal?"

"The baked chicken is delicious, as well. I'm glad you suggested this place. It's pretty new, right?"

"Gabriel's? It wasn't here eighteen years ago if that's what you're asking. Actually, it opened a few years after I returned home from medical school. The owner is a good friend of my brother Gannon so I tend to drop in occasionally."

"What made you decide to come back to Phoenix after medical school?"

And what made you stay away? As much as he wanted to ask that question, he answered hers. "I couldn't imagine living anywhere else. I missed home. I missed my family. I figured this was where I belonged. Phoenix is a beautiful city."

"Yes, it is."

"Yet you stayed away," he pointed out.

Regret darkened her eyes. "After living here all my life I figured it was time to see the world and going to school on the east coast helped. In Phoenix I was Reverend Hugh McKay's granddaughter and everyone expected me to act a certain way. In Connecticut, where no one knew me, I could be myself."

"I can't imagine you getting buck wild."

She chuckled. "I didn't go that far but I had my fun. I figured I deserved it because I studied hard. I was lucky to get a job with a top architectural firm after college in Boston. I felt my life was set."

"Then you met your ex."

He saw the regret in her gaze deepen. "Yes, then I met Carter Robinson. He worked at another firm. We met at a party and dated a year and then got married."

Tyson didn't say anything, but his mind was filled with thoughts of how different things might have been had she returned to Phoenix after college. Then maybe their paths would have crossed. *And then what?* he silently asked himself. *You aren't a serious kind of guy, never was. All you could have offered her was a romp between the sheets.* He took a sip of his water knowing that was true.

Hunter tipped her head to the side and stared at Tyson. When he wasn't trying to get a girl on her back, he was surprisingly easy to talk to. But then he very well might be so engaging just to reel her in like he'd tried doing in high school.

When the waiter came to remove the dishes she placed her briefcase on the table, opened it and pulled out her notepad. "Now for business."

"All right."

He was agreeable. She was surprised and had expected him to make some attempt to delay things. "So tell me what you would like in your house."

"Besides you in my bed?"

Now the Tyson Steele she knew had returned. "Won't happen, Tyson, so get over it."

"Doubt if I can, Hunter."

Whenever he said her name she felt a tingling sensation in the lower part of her belly. "Try real hard." With her notebook and pen in hand she forced herself back into business mode. "How many bedrooms would you like in your home?"

"At least six."

When she lifted her brow, he said, "A room for each of my brothers in case their wives ever put them out."

"At the same time?"

He shrugged. "You never know. And they're smart

enough to not to move back home. Mom would drive them to drink."

She fought back a smile. "Not your mom. I remember her from church. I was always in awe of her. She was beautiful."

"She still is beautiful. However, she does have one major flaw."

"What?" Hunter asked, taking a sip of her water.

"She likes getting into her sons' business too much to suit us. If she had her way we would all be married."

"And, of course, that's a bad thing."

"For me it is. I can't speak for my brothers since she got to three of them already."

Hunter shook her head. "I'm sure it wasn't your mom that 'got to them.' I would think it was their wives. From what I hear they fell in love."

He gave her a smile. "You're right. They're pretty damn smitten. Now they're looking at me, Mercury and Gannon like they expect us to follow suit."

"But you won't."

"I won't. I like being single."

"I bet you do. Now, to get back to your design. You want six bedrooms, one of them the master. Any specifics there?"

"Umm, I want it big and spacious. Huge windows. Large walk-in closet and the regular stuff that goes in a bedroom. Nothing far-out like what Galen has. He built a house in the mountains and his bedroom has glass walls and a glass ceiling. He likes lying in bed and looking up at the stars."

"Sounds beautiful."

"It is if that's your taste. Not mine. I want regular walls and when I lay in bed and look up the only thing I want to see is a ceiling fan."

"What about the kitchen?"

"I want a large kitchen."

She raised a brow. "You cook?"

"No. But for some reason women are impressed by the size of a man's kitchen."

She fought the urge to laugh. "Are they?"

"Yes. Some think if they get in your kitchen and cook you a good meal then you'll sweep them off their feet."

"Hasn't worked yet, I gather."

"When I sweep them off their feet I head for the bedroom and not the wedding chapel as they would like."

For some crazy reason the thought of him heading for the bedroom with any woman annoyed her. "What's the range of square footage you want?"

"Minimum of thirty-five hundred and max of fifty-five."

"That's a lot of house for a single person."

He smiled. "I figure I'll eventually have plenty of nieces and nephews and would want a big enough place for them to enjoy themselves when they come visit their uncle Tyson."

Over the next half hour Tyson continued to add on to his wish list. And there were a few things she suggested that he hadn't thought about. With additional land, a home in the country would be different from one built in the city. Already ideas were forming in her head and she couldn't wait to get started on this project.

"I think that will be enough information for now,"

she said finally, putting her notepad away. "I should have some preliminary sketches for you within a week to ten days. You can call Pauline and make an—"

"I prefer calling you directly."

"Why?"

"I just do."

"I hired Pauline for a reason."

"Tell that to your other clients."

She glared over at him. What she should do is get up, thank him for lunch and leave. But he was her client and at the moment he was the only one she had. She pulled her business card out of her purse and scribbled her mobile number on the back of it. "Don't call unless it's about business."

He took the card and slid it into his pocket while smiling at her. "I'm beginning to think you don't like me."

He didn't know how close to the truth that was. Just when she thought he might have some redeeming qualities, he proved her wrong. "Time for me to get back to the office. Thanks for lunch."

"We need to do this again. Maybe dinner the next time."

Deciding not to address Tyson's suggestion, she stood. "Goodbye, Tyson." And then she walked off. Try as she might she couldn't ignore the heat of his gaze on her back...and especially on her backside.

Chapter 5

A week and a half later, with his heart heavily weighing him down, Tyson entered his condo. Losing a patient was never easy. Although Morris Beaumont and his family had known the risks, the married father of two—and grandfather of four—had chosen to have the surgery anyway. And he hadn't survived. Delivering the news to the Beaumont family hadn't been easy. They had been hoping to beat the odds and had taken the news hard.

Tyson clenched his jaw, trying to keep his emotions at bay. Sure, he was a doctor, saw people dying every day, and accepted death as part of life. But still, doctors were human. Caring and experiencing grief didn't make one weak, as some people thought. Staying detached, as one of his professors had stressed in medical school, wasn't always easy.

Needing a beer, Tyson headed toward his kitchen to grab one out of his refrigerator. This had been a rough week with a full load of scheduled surgeries and a few unscheduled ones as well. One such emergency had been a newborn with a hole in her heart. She was doing great and if her condition continued to improve, she would be leaving the hospital and going home in another week.

Because of his workload, he hadn't followed up with Hunter, nor had she followed up with him, which probably meant she hadn't completed the initial sketches she'd talked about. Over the next number of days, which he had off, he'd get in touch with her.

The first thing on his agenda was getting laid. He needed sex like he needed this beer, he thought, popping the tab and taking a long, pleasurable gulp. He licked his lips afterward. He was beginning to feel restless and edgy. At least twenty-four hours of sleep would alleviate the former problem, but the latter would only be relieved between the legs of a woman. But not any woman. Hunter.

He took another swig of his beer. That thought filled him with concern. When had he begun lusting after just one woman? Even worse, when did his dreams just center on one woman? At night, whenever his head hit the pillow, he deliberately shut out unpleasant thoughts and only allowed his mind to conjure up pleasant ones. Hunter always headed the list.

Why was he focused on getting her to the one place

she'd made it clear she didn't want to be, which was his bed? And why did he think that once he got her there the real thing would be far better than any dream?

Tyson's cell phone rang and the ringtone indicated which brother it was. He pulled the phone off his belt. "What's up, Mercury?"

"Just checking on you. Mom told us why you didn't make last Thursday night. You okay?"

Over the years his mother had deemed Thursdays as family dinner night at their parents' home. Eden Tyson Steele expected all six of her sons to be present and accounted for, grudgingly or otherwise, unless one had a good excuse. Tyson and his brothers knew their mother used the Thursday night dinners as a way to show her sons that although their father had once been a die-hard womanizer, after meeting her all that had come to an end. She wanted them to see with their own eyes that a man like Drew Steele, who'd been known for his wild ways, could fall in love one day, marry and be true to one woman for the rest of his days. Galen, Eli and Jonas had gotten the intended message. The jury was still out for him, Mercury and Gannon. As far as Tyson was concerned, the jury could stay out for him because he wasn't changing his mind about marriage.

He was having way too much fun being single and sharing his bed with any woman he wanted.

Except for one by the name of Hunter McKay. The one he wanted with a passion.

"Tyson?"

He'd almost forgotten his brother was on the phone. "Yes, sorry. Rough stretch at work. I plan to sleep it off."

"Good idea. I'm leaving town later today for Dallas. Might have a new client with the Cowboys."

"That's good." Mercury was a former NFL player turned sports agent. He enjoyed what he did and traveled a lot.

"I thought I'd check on you before I left. By the way, I visited with the twins yesterday. They're so tiny."

Tyson figured there was no need to mention to Mercury that most newborns were. "Yes, they are. But they'll grow up fast and be walking before you know it. Getting into all kinds of stuff."

"I can't see laid-back Galen trying to keep up with them."

Neither could he, but then he hadn't figured his oldest brother would ever marry, either. "What's Gannon up to?" His youngest brother had taken over the day-to-day operations of their father's trucking company when the old man had retired a few years ago. Gannon even enjoyed getting behind a rig himself every once in a while.

"Gannon is planning to drive one of his rigs for a pickup in Florida later this week."

"That's a long ride."

"Yes, but knowing Gannon, he'll have fun along the way."

Tyson frowned. That was what worried him. While growing up, since he and Galen had been the oldest two Steeles, his parents—especially his mother—had expected them to look out for Gannon, who was the baby in the family. Although Gannon was now thirty-two, Tyson was discovering that old habits were hard to break. "I'll talk to him before he hits the road."

"It might be a good idea for you to do that. I'll talk with you later, Tyson."

"Okay and have a safe trip." Tyson clicked off the phone and returned it to his belt.

After he finished off the last of his beer, he released a throaty, testosterone-filled growl. It was a testament to how long he'd gone without a woman, which was so unlike him. He needed to step up his game, be the conqueror he knew he could be. Turn up the heat and do what he had warned Hunter he planned to do and seduce the hell out of her.

A smile touched his lips as he headed for his bedroom. First he would get the sleep he needed and then he would make it his business to seek out the object of his passion. Hunter McKay thought she'd given the last word, but he had news for her.

"Yes, and thanks for calling, Mrs. Davis. I'm looking forward to meeting you as well."

Hunter hung up the phone as a huge smile touched her lips. That would be the third new client she'd gotten in a week. It didn't even bother her that all three referrals had come from Tyson. The first, Don Jamison, was a colleague of Tyson's at the hospital. Dr. Jamison and his wife were new to town and currently living in an apartment. They had recently purchased land on the outskirts of town and were anxious to build their home.

Tessa Motley's mother was a patient of Tyson's. When she had mentioned that she and her husband planned to build a house on property that Tessa had inherited from a grandmother, Tyson had recommended Hunter.

Then there were the Davises, an older couple with dreams of building a house on beachfront property they had recently purchased in Savannah.

Hunter rose to her feet and walked over to the coffeepot to pour herself a cup. Her thoughts couldn't help but dwell on the man who'd helped to give her business a kick start. It has been two weeks since she'd seen or talked to him. She had called and left a message with him two days ago that the preliminary sketches for his house were ready. However, he hadn't bothered to call her back.

In a way she should be glad he'd given up on pursuing her, but for some reason she wasn't. Mainly because if he wasn't chasing her that meant some other woman was holding his interest now. Why did that bother her? Probably because he still managed to creep into her nightly dreams, which were getting steamier and more erotic. Going without sex for four years had finally caught up with her. Even now the thought of being seduced by Tyson Steele wasn't as unappealing as it had been originally. She took a sip of her coffee, not believing she was actually thinking that way.

She turned when she heard the knock on her door. "Come in."

The door opened and the very subject of her thoughts walked in. Tyson strode in with the casual arrogance that was so much a part of him. She was forced to admit the man was the most sensuous piece of artwork she'd ever seen. So much so it was mind-boggling. He was the last person she'd expected to see today and his surprise visit had her breathless.

He gave her a sexy smile that made her knees weaken. She could actually feel the sexual chemistry sizzling between them. "Hunter."

The sound of his voice actually made her skin tingle. What were the odds that the very man she'd been thinking about suddenly appeared? How strange was that? Somehow she found her voice to ask. "Tyson? What are you doing here?"

"I got the message you left on my phone."

"That was two days ago." She hoped he hadn't heard the testiness in her voice.

"I know. I slept for almost two days."

Hunter fought back the temptation to ask the question that burned in her mind. *With whom?* Instead she put her coffee cup down and moved to stand in front of her desk. She felt the heat of his gaze with every step she took. Every other time, the fact that he closely watched her every move had annoyed her, but not now. It thrilled her.

When she reached her desk she turned and looked over at him to find his piercing green eyes staring her up and down. She fought back a heated shiver and asked, "Is anything wrong?"

"What makes you think something is wrong, Hunter?"

She wished it didn't do things to her whenever he said her name. "You're staring." She'd worn a dress today and his gaze continued to roam up and down her legs.

"I am, aren't I? My only excuse is that you're good to look at."

Carter had rarely given her compliments, so hearing them from Tyson definitely boosted her feminine confidence. He might be checking her out but she was doing the same with him. She couldn't help but appreciate how good he looked in his jeans and the way his shirt fit over his well-toned muscles. She forced her eyes away. "I'm sure that's a line you've used on a number of women."

"No. It's not."

Deciding not to believe him, she looked past his shoulder to the door. "How did you get into my office without Pauline announcing you?"

He shrugged. "I told her she didn't have to bother. I like announcing myself. Besides, she was packing up to leave, and she told me to tell you that she would see you Monday morning."

Hunter glanced at her watch. She hadn't realized it was so late. That meant they were alone and that wasn't a good thing right now with her present frame of mind. The best thing was to send him packing. Picking up the manila folder off her desk, she offered it to him. "Here's what you came for."

Tyson moved toward her with calm, deliberate strides, and when he came to a stop directly in front of her, she tried ignoring the sparks going off inside her. Instead of accepting the folder, he reached out and brushed the tips of his fingers across her cheek. "That's not what I came for, Hunter. This is."

And before she could draw her next breath, he leaned in and captured her mouth with his.

* * *

Tyson hadn't lied when he'd told Hunter that this was what he'd come for. He refused to suffer through another dream where he'd kissed her madly without getting a taste of the real thing. And now he was discovering that no dream could compare. It didn't come close.

He'd known when he took her mouth that he risked getting his tongue bitten off. Evidently she needed this kiss as much as he did if the way her tongue was mating with his was anything to go by. He could taste her hunger in this kiss, and he could feel the passion and the desire engulfing them. He was greedily lapping up her mouth.

He'd kissed her once before, years ago behind the lockers at school. It had been way too short and at the time he hadn't known how to use his tongue like he did now. He hadn't known how much kissing could thoroughly arouse a man when done the right way and with the right woman.

Tyson wrapped his arms around Hunter's waist to bring her closer. Never had any woman's mouth tasted so delicious, so hot that it was heating the blood rushing through his veins. In seconds he had her purring and himself moaning.

He heard the folder she'd been holding fall to the floor seconds before she wrapped her arms around his neck as he continued to feast on her mouth. He moaned again when he felt her hardened nipples press into his chest. And if that wasn't bad enough, her scent was all around him, seducing him in a way no other woman had ever been capable of doing.

He knew this kiss was the beginning and was determined for it not to be the end. He had succeeded in breaking through her shell, but it was imperative not to push too hard and too soon. So he did what he really didn't want to do—pull back from the kiss.

Before she could say anything—he was certain it would be something he didn't want to hear right then—he leaned close and whispered against her moist lips. "Have dinner with me, Hunter."

Hunter could only stand there, feeling weak in the knees, while she gazed into the green eyes staring back at her. One minute Tyson had been standing in front of her and the next he had his tongue in her mouth. And the minute she tasted it she was powerless to resist him.

His kiss had been possessive. It had sent her emotions in a tailspin, accelerating out of control. At the time, something had convinced her that she desperately needed the urgent mating of his tongue with hers and she'd given in to it. Now that the kiss was over, common sense had returned and she was thinking more rationally. At least she hoped so.

"Hunter?"

She drew in a deep breath. He had asked her to have dinner with him and there was no way she could do that, especially after that kiss. He had shown her what could happen if she lowered her guard with him just for one moment. "I can't have dinner with you."

He frowned down at her. "You can't or you won't?"

It was basically the same thing in her book. "Does it matter?"

"Yes."

"Not to me, Tyson."

"What are you afraid of?"

That question irked her. "I'm not afraid of anything."

He crossed his arms over his chest. "Do you know what I think?"

"Not really."

"I'm going to tell you anyway. I think you're afraid that I have the capability to make you feel like a woman again."

Hunter swallowed deeply, knowing what he said was true, but she'd never admit to him. "Sorry to disappointment you but—"

"You could never disappoint me, Hunter. Only pleasure me."

If his words were meant to take the wind from her sails, they succeeded. She wished he wouldn't say things like that. Words that could slice through her common sense and make her want things she shouldn't have. "Doesn't matter."

"It does to me. Let's have dinner and talk about it."

That was the last thing she wanted to do—discuss how she'd come unglued in his arms. "I'd rather not."

"I wish you would. What I told you earlier was true. I've been sleeping for almost forty-eight hours."

"Why?"

"A lot of surgeries at the hospital." He paused a moment and then added, "And I lost one of my patients during surgery last week."

His words sliced through her irritation. "Oh, Tyson,

I'm so sorry to hear that." Without realizing she was doing so, she reached out and touched his arm.

He drew in a deep breath. "Doctors aren't superheroes and we can only do so much but…"

"But you did your best."

"Yes," he agreed somberly. "I did my best. Unfortunately for Mr. Beaumont, my best wasn't good enough."

A part of Hunter understood how Tyson was feeling. All she had to do was to recall that time when her grandfather had first taken ill. She had been at the hospital with him when a commotion out in the hall had drawn her attention. She'd stepped out in time to hear some family member of a person who'd just died accuse the doctor of not doing enough. The doctor had tried to calm the person down, saying he'd done all he could. Hunter had known the accusations hurled at the doctor had hurt. For a quick second she'd seen the agonized look in the doctor's eyes. And then she'd understood. The man was a doctor but he was also a human being. Just like family members grieved for their lost loved ones, doctors grieved for the patients they lost.

Tyson leaned down to pick up the folder she had dropped earlier. When he handed it to her, he said, "Look, I didn't mean to mention that. I asked you to dinner, not to attend a pity party."

"I'm glad because a pity party isn't what you're going to get. If the offer for dinner still stands, then I'll take it."

He eyed her curiously. "Why did you change your mind?"

"Because although you have the ability to irritate

me, I do need to go over these with you," she said, handing the folder back to him. "And I really should be nice to you."

At the sensual gleam that suddenly appeared in his eyes, she quickly said, "Not *that* nice."

He chuckled. "And why do you think you should be nice to me?"

"Thanks to you, I have three new clients. I appreciate the referrals."

Tyson shrugged. "No big deal."

"It's my business we're talking about, so to me it is a big deal. Thank you."

"You're welcome. But there's one thing I forgot to mention about dinner."

She looked up at him. "What?"

"It's at my place."

She frowned, not liking how he'd easily maneuvered that one. There was no way he could have forgotten to mention that earlier. "I thought you couldn't cook."

"I can't," he said, heading for the door. "But I know how to pick up takeout. I hope you like Thai food."

Hunter did, but she wasn't sure having dinner at his place was a smart idea. She was about to tell him so when he added over his shoulder, "I'll text you my address. See you in an hour."

And then he opened the door and walked out, closing it behind him.

Chapter 6

Hunter stared at the closed door and a part of her wished there was more going on between her and Tyson than physical attraction. The sexual vibes they emitted whenever they were together were so strong she bet a person walking across the street could pick up on it.

And that kiss…

Just thinking about it made her weak in the knees so she moved around her desk and sat down. The kiss had started off gentle and when she began participating, mingling her tongue with his, it had gotten downright passionate to a degree she'd never experienced before. Who kissed like that? Evidently Tyson Steele did. She didn't recall the one time they'd kissed back in high school having this type of effect on her. He had definitely gotten experience over the years. The man knew how to use his tongue in a way that could be destructive to a woman's mind. It had definitely obliterated her common sense. For a minute there she hadn't wanted him to stop and had been disappointed when he'd done so.

The kiss had evidently affected him, too. She had been able to feel the heat radiating from his body as he kissed her. And when she had wrapped her arms around his neck and pressed her body closer to his, she had felt evidence of his desire. His huge erection had pressed into her middle and all she could think about was how it would feel inside her.

Like in her dreams.

Hunter drew in a deep breath. That kiss had gotten out of hand, and on top of that, she had agreed to have dinner with him at his place. What could she have been thinking? Tyson had told her what he wanted from her and now he probably thought it was within his reach. That was the last thing she wanted him to think.

Hunter was about to pull her cell phone out of her purse to call Tyson and cancel dinner when it rang. She frowned when she recognized the ringtone. Why would Nadine Robinson be calling her? She hadn't talked to her mother-in-law in over two years. Not since Hunter had filed for a divorce. Carter's father, Lewis Robinson, had forbidden the family from having anything to do with Hunter for divorcing his son.

Curiosity got the best of her so she clicked on the phone. "Yes, Nadine?"

"Hunter? Glad I was able to reach you. I was afraid you had changed your number."

It was on the tip of Hunter's tongue to say although she hadn't changed her phone number, she had blocked certain callers from getting through, like Nadine's son. She would have blocked Nadine's number as well, but figured the older woman had no reason to ever call her.

"This is a surprise, Nadine. What can I do for you?" Hunter decided to get straight to the point. There was no reason for her and the woman to engage in friendly chitchat.

"I called to warn you. About Carter."

Hunter lifted a brow. "Why would you want to warn me about Carter?"

"His world is falling apart. He's losing clients right and left and several employees have quit."

That didn't surprise Hunter. Although Carter had underhandedly taken her clients away, she figured it was only a matter of time before he lost them. As for the employees, although Carter was a pretty good architect, he lacked people skills, so that wasn't a shocker.

"That's not my problem, Nadine."

"I know, but he intends to make it your problem."

Hunter drew in a breath. "And how does he think he can do that?"

"I overheard him and Lewis talking. They've come up with a plan for you to return to Boston and get back with Carter."

When hell freezes over. Hunter sat up straight in her chair. "What plan?"

"Carter will be in Phoenix on business in a few weeks and he plans to look you up when he gets there. He told Lewis he will apologize to you for all he's done, tell you how much he regrets losing you and that he can't live without you. The plan is to tug on your heart-strings."

"My heartstrings?"

"Yes."

Hunter raised a brow. "What does my heart have to do with it?"

"Because you're still in love with him."

Hunter shook her head. Now she had heard every-thing. "Nadine, why would anyone think I'm still in love with Carter?"

"Because you haven't been seriously involved with anyone since your divorce. You didn't date when you were here in Boston and from what Carter is hearing, you haven't dated anyone since you've moved back to Phoenix."

Hunter frowned. "And how can he know that?"

There was a pause on the line before Nadine said, "Carter has friends in Phoenix and they occasionally report back to him on your activities. You're not in-volved with anyone so it seems you're still carrying a torch for him."

"Well, whoever thinks that is dead wrong."

"I'm glad. I was getting worried. You did the right thing by ending your marriage to my son."

Hunter frowned. "That's not what you told me, Na-dine."

"I know. But trust me, I did you a favor. I saw what was happening and refused to let you become a mini-me. Carter had begun treating you like Lewis treated me. You had started believing the lies and accepting his behavior.

I knew you deserved better. The best thing you did was divorce my son. He's out of your life and I hope you won't let him back in."

Hunter hated admitting it, but Nadine was right. She had started letting Carter get away with murder and he knew it. Instead of divorcing him, for two years she had bought into his crap that her life would be nothing without him. She'd opted to stay married to him but moved into the guest bedroom.

It had been goodbye and good riddance to Carter Robinson. And that's the way she would keep it.

"Trust me, Nadine, there's no way I will ever get back with Carter. And if he has this bizarre delusion that I'm still in love with him then he is dead wrong."

"Good. I'm glad you moved back to Phoenix. But you need to get involved with someone. You need a life. As long as you don't have one, Carter is going to think he has a chance with you again."

As far as Hunter was concerned, Nadine had no right to tell her what she needed. And Carter could think whatever he wanted. "Let me assure you, Nadine, I do have a life."

"So you're seeing someone?"

Tyson's image suddenly came into her mind. "Yes, I am seeing someone. In fact I'll be meeting him for dinner in a couple of hours." What she'd just said hadn't been a total lie.

"I'm glad. I know you probably won't ever forgive me for siding against you during the divorce, but I did what I felt I had to do for your own good. Goodbye,

Hunter. I wish you the best and hope your young man makes you happy."

"Goodbye, Nadine."

Hunter clicked off the phone, shaking her head. Carter actually thought he could show up in Phoenix with a plan to get her back? Did he really think she was pining away for him just because she hadn't gotten seriously involved with anyone since their divorce?

At that moment her phone rang and she recognized Mo's ringtone. She was glad it wasn't Nadine calling her back. "Yes, Mo?"

"Kat called earlier. She has a date and Eric decided to come to town this weekend. Just wanted to make sure you'd be okay."

She shook her head. "You guys don't have to keep me company like I don't have a life, you know." At that moment Hunter realized she had lied to Nadine because in all honesty, she really didn't have a life.

"Mo, can I ask you something?"

"Sure."

"Do you think I'm still in love with Carter?"

There was a pause. "To be honest with you, the thought had crossed my mind a time or two. Where did that question come from?"

Hunter let out a deep sigh and told Mo about her conversation with Carter's mother. "How can you or anyone think I still care for him, Mo?"

"Well, it has been two years, Hunter, and you haven't as much as dated another man."

"The first year after my divorce I swore off men," she said, unable to keep the bitterness out of her voice.

"That's understandable."

Hunter knew that the reason Mo had divorced her ex hadn't been about another woman but about Larry's gambling addiction. When he had refused help and had sold every single item in their home to feed his habit, Mo had had enough.

"What about now since you've moved back to Phoenix?" Mo asked, interrupting Hunter's thoughts.

"I'm busy trying to start my business here."

"Then you need to learn how to multitask. And to be honest, it sounds to me like you're making excuses. Being in a relationship with someone won't consume that much of your time, Hunter. You've even got one of those Bad News Steeles hot on your tail. Do you know how many women in town would love to be in your shoes?"

"Then let them. I prefer not to do casual relationships."

"After what Carter put you through do you honestly prefer a serious one? All you'll get is nothing but heartache… unless you're entertaining the thought of marrying again."

"Never!"

"Then what's wrong with casual? I'm not saying you should start hopping from bed to bed or that you should get involved with Tyson Steele but…" Mo trailed off.

"But what?"

"If I was going to do casual after going without sex for as long as you have, Tyson would be my man. One night with him would probably make you realize what you're missing. You claim you haven't had an orgasm in so long that you've forgotten how it feels. That's sad for any single woman to admit to…unless you're doing the celibate thing."

"No, that's not it."

"Then what is it? I can see why Carter thinks you're still carrying a torch for him. What you need to do is declare your sexual independence."

"My sexual independence?"

"Yes, and I think the ideal person to start with is Tyson. The word *serious* is not in his vocabulary so you're safe there. And if the rumors about him are true, he'll make you remember just how explosive an orgasm can be and have you screaming all over the place. He told you that he had plans to seduce you, so let him."

"If I were to do that, then I become just another notch on his belt. I didn't want that when we were in high school and I don't want that now."

"Then what do you want?"

Hunter should be woman enough to admit she wanted Tyson. She couldn't help but want him after all those erotic dreams she'd been having of him lately. But she didn't want him on his terms and told Mo how she felt.

"In that case then why not take the initiative and seduce *him*? That way you'll maintain control."

Hunter gazed out her window and stared at the mountains in the distance. The sun was going down and cast a purple glow on the skyline. "Seducing a man might be easy for you, Mo, but it wouldn't be for me." She just could not see herself using her feminine wiles to get a man in bed.

Mo intruded on her thoughts. "For once will you accept that you're a woman who has needs like the rest of us? A woman who's capable of planning her own seduction and doesn't need Tyson Steele to plan it for her?" She blew out an exasperated breath. "There's no manual detailing how to go about it. You do what comes natural."

"What comes natural?"

"Yes, and it's easier than you think. There's physical attraction between you and Tyson, as well as strong sexual chemistry. Kat and I felt it that night at the club. All you have to do is let that chemistry be your guide."

Mo's words echoed in Hunter's mind long after they ended the phone call. They haunted her as she began closing her office for the weekend, knowing she had little time to decide just how she would handle Tyson. Her conversations with Nadine and Mo had made her realize it was past time to take control of her life. For a change, she needed to do whatever pleased her.

An image of Tyson suddenly appeared in her head. The thought of sharing a bed with him sent heated shivers through her body. And if he was really a master in the bedroom, as those rumors went, then he was just what she needed. In fact, he was long overdue. However, like she'd told Mo, she had one big issue with Tyson. He'd already planned how he intended for things between them to end—with his seduction of her. He probably had a spot in his bed with her name on it—right along with all those other women he'd had sex with in that same bed.

What man targets a woman for seduction and, worse, is arrogant enough to tell her, as if it's a gift she should appreciate? Only a man with the mind-set of Tyson Steele.

She would just love to best him at his own game and still get something out of it. It was about time some woman knocked him off his high horse. It would serve him right for being so darn egotistical. Could that woman be her? It would mean her stepping into a role she'd never played before, but it would be well worth it if she got the results she wanted and on her terms.

Moments later she left her office, deciding that tonight she would not allow Tyson to seduce her. She would be seducing him.

Tyson smiled as he gazed around his kitchen and dining-room areas. His sister-in-law Brittany would be proud of him. The table was set perfectly. Brittany owned Etiquette Matters, a school that taught etiquette and manners. Tyson's mother was into all that etiquette stuff and although she'd made sure they had impeccable manners while growing up, she felt her sons needed to take a refresher course. When Brittany opened a school in Phoenix after marrying Galen, Eden Tyson Steele strongly suggested that her sons enroll in one of Brittany's classes. To pacify their mother, they had.

Tyson checked his watch and drew in a deep breath, not wanting to think about this being a first for him. He didn't prepare dinner for women. They prepared dinner for him. Although he hadn't actually prepared this one, he had invited her to his place and would be feeding her. He had crossed plenty of boundaries with Hunter and wasn't sure what he should do about it.

Hell, he wasn't even sure he wanted to do anything about it. And that in itself was crazy. Why was there such strong sexual chemistry between them? What exactly had brought it on and when would it end? He had tried to recall the exact moment he'd lost his head. Had it been the moment he'd seen her when she had walked into Notorious? Or had it been when he'd conversed with her while sitting at her table? Or had it been when he'd dropped in on her unexpectedly that first time at her office? Or had it been when he'd kissed her? All he knew was that if he wasn't careful, she could easily get under his skin and he refused to let that happen.

Why was she making his plan of seduction so damn difficult? She wanted him as much as he wanted her, he was sure of it. But she continued to deny what they both wanted—one night in his bed. Was that too much to ask? He didn't think so, but evidently she did.

His phone rang, nearly startling him out of his reverie. He recognized the ringtone. It was Gannon. He picked up his cell phone from the kitchen counter. "It took you long enough to call me back, Gannon."

He could hear his youngest brother's chuckle. "Now that Galen's married, am I supposed to report in with you now?"

Gannon was becoming such a smart-ass. "Wouldn't hurt."

"Don't hold your breath, Tyson. What's up?"

"I hear you're driving one of your rigs to Florida."

"That's right. Do you want to go along for the ride?"

He'd done it before and had to admit he had fun.

The women they'd met along the way had been worth it. "Wish I could but I can't."

For some reason he didn't want to leave Phoenix right now. He refused to believe Hunter McKay had anything to do with it. Hadn't he gone two weeks without seeing her? He forced the thought to the back of his mind just how miserable those days had been.

"Too much is going on at the hospital, Gannon," he added. "I was lucky to get this time off." And he was spending it with a woman who wasn't sharing his bed. How crazy was that?

"I dropped by and saw Brittany and the twins today."

"How are they?"

"Everybody's fine. Galen was changing Ethan's diaper. Can you imagine that?"

"No, but he's a father now and with it comes responsibilities. Keep that in mind if you get it into your head to invite some woman into your rig for the night."

Gannon chuckled. "Please don't cover the birds and bees with me again, Tyson. I got it the last time."

"Just make sure you remember it. And stay condom safe."

"Whatever. I'm headed out in the morning. I just left the folks' place and they're still beaming over the twins. Mom has taken over a thousand pictures already."

"Doesn't surprise me."

At that moment Tyson's doorbell sounded. "My dinner guest has arrived. I'll talk to you later."

"Dinner guest? You can't cook."

"Not trying to cook," he said, moving around the breakfast bar to head for the door.

"I can't believe you invited a woman to your place."

Tyson rolled his eyes. "Women have been to my place before, Gannon. Numerous times."

"As a bedmate. Not a dinner guest."

He didn't need his brother reminding him of his strange behavior. "Be safe on the road."

"Okay. See you in a week."

"Will do," Tyson said, clicking off the phone and sliding it into the back pocket of his jeans. He stopped in the middle of his living room and inhaled deeply, convinced he could pick up Hunter's scent through the door. He shook his head. He had to be imagining things.

He glanced around his condo again. Although he appreciated his cleaning lady, she never had a lot to do because he spent most of his time at the hospital. But still, he was glad he wasn't a slob and kept a pretty tidy place. Hunter ought to be impressed.

Tyson shuddered at where his thoughts had gone again. Who cared if she was impressed or not? A completely physical, emotion-free involvement was what he wanted with Hunter. Inviting her to dinner was a means to an end, and the end was getting her into his bed.

He walked to the door, opened it and faltered at the same time he was certain his jaw dropped. He could only stand there and stare wide-eyed. What in the world...?

"I hope I'm not late, Tyson."

He inhaled sharply as deep-seated hunger nearly took control of his senses. Hunter had changed clothes. The coral dress she was wearing now fitted her body like another layer of skin, showing every single curve.

The neckline dipped low at just the right angle to show enough of her breasts, while at the same time enticing him to want to see more. She always looked totally feminine in whatever outfit she wore, but in this particular dress she looked like sex on two legs. And speaking of legs... They looked even more gorgeous in this short dress with a pair of killer heels on her feet. The entire ensemble was meant to push a man's buttons and it was pushing his in a big way. Somehow she'd transformed her image from a good girl to a totally naughty one.

For a moment he couldn't say anything. His mind filled with thoughts of just how he would take this dress off her later. He fought the urge to do it now. He was tempted to reach out and touch her all over to see if the material of her dress felt as sensuous as it looked. Instead he stood there, leaning against the doorjamb while his gaze roamed up and down her body, appreciating every stitch, inch and curve he saw.

"Tyson, I hope I'm not late."

She repeated herself so he figured it was time to rein in his desire and respond. "You're right on time."

And with the feel of his erection pressing hard against the zipper of his jeans, he meant every single word. "Come in," he invited, moving aside.

She entered, walking past him. He appreciated the sway of her hips and how her every step placed emphasis on her delectable-looking backside, as well as those killer heels on her feet. And if that wasn't mind-boggling enough, her delicious scent almost made him moan.

"Thanks for inviting me to dinner," she said, turning around in the middle of his foyer.

Hell, he would invite her to dinner every single night if she showed up looking like this. If she bent over even just a little he was certain he would be able to see her panties. That thought made his erection even harder.

Lust began taking over his mind, drugging him, gripping him, and he hoped he could make it through dinner. After that the night would belong to him and he intended to make good use of his time. She had to have known wearing this outfit would increase his desire for her. He wanted her so badly his entire body ached.

"No need to thank me," he said, leading her to the living room. He wished they could skip dinner altogether and head straight to the bedroom.

"We're having Thai, right?"

He turned and his gaze automatically went to her legs. He could envision her doing a lot with those legs and all of them included him between them. He forced his gaze from her legs up to her face. Why did her lips look like they needed to be kissed? "Sorry. What did you ask?"

Hunter smiled at him. "I asked if we're still having Thai."

She might be having Thai but he was having her. "Yes. The table is all set and the food is ready."

"Good. I'm starving."

So was he. So were his hands. His fingers. His mouth. His shaft. All were anxious to touch her. Taste her. Get inside her.

Tyson drew in a deep breath, trying to get back the control he was quickly losing. She had a lot of guts wearing this outfit to his place tonight. Had she thought he would focus on dinner and not on her? Especially when he'd warned her of his plans to seduce her?

Wait a minute... Warning bells began going off in his head. This whole thing was too good to be true. Why did he smell a setup? Tyson crossed his arms over his chest. "Okay, Hunter. What's going on? Why are you dressed like this?"

She lifted a brow. "Dressed like what?"

"Like you'll be my dessert once we finish dinner."

Chapter 7

Hunter took a deep breath, trying to ignore the intense nervousness floating around in her stomach. What had Mo said about just doing what came naturally? If that was the case then why was she suddenly feeling like a fish out of water? Now she was wondering if she'd overdone things, especially with this outfit. She had dropped by Phase One, a boutique she'd passed several times on her way home. A twentysomething salesgirl had been more than happy to help her shop for the perfect seduction outfit.

"So, do you intend on being my dessert, Hunter?"

She licked her lips and saw his gaze follow the movement of her tongue. "Your dessert?"

"Yes." Dropping his hands, he closed the distance

separating them. "Do I need to go into details? What about a demonstration?"

She wished his eyes didn't captivate her, or that huge erection she couldn't help but notice didn't hold such promise. When he'd covered the distance separating them, he did so with the ease of a hunter stalking his prey. She had a mind to take a step back, but decided to stand her ground. "Neither is necessary, Tyson. Do you have a problem with what I'm wearing?"

A smile curved the corner of his lips. "No, I don't have a problem with it, as long as you know what it means."

"And what does it mean?"

A serious smile touched his lips. "A woman wears a dress like this to give a man a sign as to how the evening will end."

"I suggest you don't jump to conclusions. I merely decided to change into something more comfortable. But if my dress makes you uncomfortable then…"

"Doesn't bother me as long as you know I'll be trying like hell to get you out of it later."

"Do you always say whatever you want?"

"No need to play games when it comes to us. I told you my plans for you that first night. Now, let's enjoy dinner."

Hunter drew in a deep breath. Tyson Steele might think he had his own plan, but he would find out soon enough she also had hers.

As he led her over to the dining room table and pulled out a chair for her, she looked around. "You have a nice home, Tyson. It's pretty spacious for a condo. The architect in me likes the layout. I have a fondness for the open floor plan. Great for entertaining."

He shrugged. "I don't consider it as home. Since I spend a lot of time at the hospital, I think of this as the place where I eat and sleep."

Hunter figured he could have said that this was the place where he ate, slept and had sex. She figured he had a revolving door to his bedroom.

She couldn't help noticing how nice he'd set the table. Fine china and silverware, cloth napkins and crystal glasses. "Pretty fancy for takeout."

He leaned close and stared into her eyes as he poured wine into her glass. "Thought I'd impress you."

"You have."

"Good. I'll be back with everything in a second."

Hunter didn't release the breath she'd been holding until he left to go into the kitchen.

Tyson decided not to question his luck tonight. Hunter could pretend indifference all she wanted, but there had to be a reason she'd worn that dress. She was a very sensual woman and tonight he was very much aware of her body, more so than ever in that outfit.

Gathering all the dishes, he left the kitchen to re-enter the dining room and she glanced in his direction. "Need help?"

"No, I got this," he said, placing several platters and serving utensils in the middle of the table. He quickly returned to the kitchen to grab the bowl of tossed salad, the only thing he could actually claim he'd made. "I love Thai, and Latti's makes it just the way I like. Red roast duck on rice is my favorite. I think you'll enjoy it."

"I'm sure I will. It looks delicious."

"Then let's dig in," he said, taking the chair across from her.

"Umm, why don't you serve me?"

He glanced over at her. "Serve you?"

"Yes," she said, holding up her plate expectantly.

He held her gaze for a moment before picking up the serving spoon and proceeded to place several spoonfuls into her plate. What the hell was going on here? When did he serve women? He forced back his irritation and figured he would get his just reward later that night.

She took a forkful and moaned. Then she licked her lips.

Tyson felt a tightening in his groin as he watched her. He would serve her food again if she licked her lips like that one more time. It had him remembering the kisses they'd shared. Made him anticipate the ones he intended to share later.

"This is delicious, Tyson."

Why did her compliment make his chest expand? It's not like he'd cooked it himself. "Glad you think so."

For the next few minutes they ate in silence. Instead of using the quiet to his advantage to regroup and make sure he was back in control of his senses, he found himself becoming even more aware of her. Like that cute tiny mole just below her right ear. Why hadn't he noticed that before?

"I guess I really was starving."

Her words made him look at her plate. It was clean.

Mercury swore that a woman who had a healthy appetite when it came to food also had a healthy appetite in the bedroom. Tyson never noticed a correlation, but tonight he was hoping there was one. "I guess you were. Want seconds?"

"Don't tempt me."

He didn't see why he shouldn't when she was definitely tempting him. It wouldn't take much to clear this table and proceed to spread her across it. "I won't tempt you. Would you like more wine?"

"Yes."

He could have poured the wine from where he sat but decided now was the time to make his move. He walked around the table to stand beside her and poured the wine into her glass. "I hope you left room for dessert."

She looked up at him and held his gaze. He could feel her need even if she was trying to downplay it. She wanted him as much as he wanted her. He knew the signs. He could see it in her eyes. Desire was lining her pupils, drenching her irises. The nipples of her breasts had formed into tight buds and were pressing against her dress. But the telltale sign was her feminine scent. The aroma was getting to him and he didn't want to play games if playing those games would delay things. He was ready to take things from the dining room straight into the bedroom.

He watched her tongue when she nervously licked her top lip. "I guess this is where we need to talk, Tyson."

Talk? The only talking they needed to do was pillow talk and that would come later. "What do we need to talk about?"

Instead of answering him, she picked up her glass and took a sip of her wine. She placed the glass back down and held his gaze once again. "About your misconception that if I sleep with you tonight it will because you seduced me into doing so."

He didn't see it as a misconception, but as a fact. "Do you have a problem with me seducing you, Hunter?"

She nodded. "Yes, I have a problem with it. I refuse to be just another one of your conquests."

Tyson hoped history wasn't repeating itself. If he recalled, she'd said something similar eighteen years ago. Back then she wanted to be his one and only girl. Surely she wasn't asking for some sort of commitment from him, because if she was she wouldn't be getting it.

He hated to ask but really needed to know. "And just what do you want to be?"

"The one doing the seducing."

"Why?"

Hunter had expected Tyson's question. "I told you. Because I refuse to be another one of your conquests. That night at Notorious you stated you plan to seduce me. If we sleep together tonight, I don't want you to think you've succeeded. I want to set the record straight that if we share a bed it will be because it was my choice and not because you've done or said anything to persuade or entice me."

"So you want to play a mind game?" Tyson asked.

"No. I don't want to play any games. I just don't want you thinking that like all those other women, I fell under your spell. I can get up and walk out the door right now if that's what I choose to do. There's no way you can touch me, kiss me or talk to me that will make me change my mind unless it's something I want to do."

An arrogant smile touched his lips. "You think not?"

"I know not."

"You wouldn't be the first woman who thought so. But fine," he said, taking a step back. "If you want to seduce me, go right ahead. Don't expect me to resist. It will be a first."

Hunter lifted a brow. "No woman has ever seduced you before?"

"No. If a woman wants me and I'm not interested in her, no amount of seduction on her part will make me change my mind. And if it's a woman I want, they usually fit into two categories. Those who are willing and those who aren't."

He paused a minute as if to make sure she was keeping up with his logic. "Now, if it's a willing woman then there's no need for seduction because getting together will be mutual."

"And if she's unwilling?" she asked.

An egotistical smile touched his lips. "Those are few, but any woman who resists my interest just needs a little coaxing. That's when my seduction comes into play. And just so you know, I'm an expert at it."

He was conceited enough to believe that, Hunter thought. She figured he classified her in the latter group, which was why he'd put his plan of seduction in place. "And you thought I needed coaxing?"

"Yes. But I can always move you to the willing category if it makes you feel better."

Hunter frowned. He just didn't get it. She wanted sleeping with him to be her choice and not his. She didn't want to be just another woman seduced by Tyson Steele. She stood and said, "I think I need to go. Dinner was great and—"

"Wait." He stared at her while he shoved his hands into the pockets of his jeans. "What's going on, Hunter? What is this about?"

"Nothing is going on. I've simply changed my mind about seducing you. I suggest you do the same."

"What are you afraid of, Hunter?"

She lifted her chin. "What makes you think I'm afraid of anything?"

"Because you're running."

He was right. She was running. "You want to seduce me and I won't let you. I want to seduce you, but you don't think I can. So what's the point?"

"I didn't say I didn't think you could seduce me. I merely stated no woman ever felt the need to try because I've always picked the women I wanted." He looked back at her, stared at her as if she was a puzzle he was trying to figure out. Then he added, "I want you, so it doesn't matter to me who seduces whom."

"It does to me."

"I see that and I'm trying to understand why."

She forced her gaze away from him and knew there was no way she could explain it to him. All this was a game to Tyson, a game he intended to win, and if he seduced her then he would be winning. It was just like with Carter. He'd played games with her for eight years. She'd been a contestant with no chance of winning, not even his heart. And God knows she'd tried. Well, those days were over and now she flat-out refused to let any man best her ever again.

But she couldn't possibly get Tyson to understand her past. "It's too complicated to explain."

"Try me," he said, reaching out and touching her arm.

She drew in a sharp breath at his touch. And held it when he slowly caressed her skin, making tingles of desire spread through her.

"And try this," he added, leaning forward and using the tip of his tongue to lick her lips. "And I would just love for you to try this," he whispered, deliberately pressing his body closer to hers so that she could feel his hard erection against the juncture of her thighs.

"You're trying to seduce me," she accused in a breathless whisper and could feel herself getting weak in the knees. Resisting him in his domain would be harder than she thought.

"I'm showing you that we want each other, Hunter. The desire is mutual. You can arouse me just as much as I can arouse you. So why does it matter who's seducing whom?"

A part of Hunter knew it shouldn't but for her it did. "It matters to me, Tyson. I refuse to be seduced by you."

He paused a moment before releasing her and taking a step back. "Fine. Since it matters so much to you, then go ahead. Seduce the hell out of me."

Tyson wasn't sure what was going on with Hunter, but he figured it had something to do with her ex. She wouldn't be the first woman who'd brought baggage into his bedroom. And on more than one occasion he'd allowed them to do so knowing that after his first thrust into their body, whatever issues they were dealing with would take a backseat to the pleasures they would experience in his bed.

Hunter was being difficult and he didn't need a difficult woman. So why was he even putting up with it? And why, even now, did he want her more than he'd ever wanted any woman? He shook his head. Because she was the "one who got away." All it would take was one night of tumbling between the sheets with her to get her out of his system. Hell, he probably didn't need the entire night. A few hours should work just fine.

As he watched her gaze sweep him up and down, he knew she was aware of his arousal. He refused to waste this opportunity to get her into his bed. "Do it, Hunter," he whispered hoarsely. "Seduce me."

For the longest time they stared at each other and then she took a tentative step closer, reducing the distance between them. Standing on tiptoes, she slanted her mouth across his.

Holy hell, Tyson thought the moment she slid her tongue inside his mouth. At that moment he wasn't sure what was getting to him more—the way her tongue was overpowering his mouth, or the feel of her hardened nipples pressed against his chest. He thought he could just stand there and let her use his mouth to work out whatever issue she was dealing with. But he soon discovered his desire for Hunter went deeper than that.

There was no way he could ignore the erratic pounding of his heart or the insistent way his erection pressed against his zipper. He fought back a moan and then another, and when she shifted her body to meld it even closer to his, he wrapped his arms around her waist. She continued to take his mouth in a way that rocked him to his core. He'd kissed, and been kissed, by scores of women, but it wasn't just Hunter's kiss that had him weak in the knees. It was her taste. Her personal flavor had blood rushing fast and furious through his veins even as he shivered on the inside.

Then suddenly she broke off the kiss. "I want to finish this," she said in a raspy tone, licking her lips.

His gut clenched. He wanted to finish this, as well. Tyson was about to suggest they go into his bedroom when she began moving toward his living room. "Hey, my bedroom is this way," he said.

She looked over her shoulder. "Yours may be but mine is not."

He frowned, wondering what the hell she was talking about. He got even more confused when she grabbed her purse off his sofa. She turned around and said, "I can't share a bed with you here."

"What?" he asked, mystified.

She placed the strap of her purse on her shoulder. "I can't share the bed that others have shared with you."

He stared at her and saw the seriousness in the dark eyes staring back at him. "Why?"

"This is my plan of seduction and I want to finish it at my place. In my own bed. Not one you've shared with a zillion others."

No other woman had ever made such a bold request. He would not have allowed it. So why was he allowing it now? And why was she concerned with how many women had slept in his bed? It was *his* bed and he claimed all rights to it. And for her information, not all his conquests had been brought back here. He'd taken a few to a hotel. But, he admitted only to himself, he rarely went to a woman's home. Very rarely.

Tyson knew men handled things differently when it came to having sex with women. Some didn't invite women to their home, saying it felt like the woman was invading their personal space. Galen and his cousin Donovan Steele from Charlotte had both had the same mind-set in their bachelor days. Tyson never had a problem with it because any woman that he had sex with here knew not to return without an invitation.

"I'm leaving." Hunter turned and headed for the door.

He stared as she walked away, not missing that backside he'd made plans to ride and those gorgeous legs he'd intended to slide between. What in the hell had gone wrong? One part of him wanted to think her leaving was for the best because she certainly thought a lot of herself if she assumed she could call the shots. But another part, the one determined to have sex with her regardless of whose bed he did it in, overruled his common sense, and so he asked, "What's your address?"

She rattled it off over her shoulder. When she reached his door she turned around. "I'll be waiting, Tyson."

"You won't be waiting long." He barely got the words out before she opened the door and closed it shut behind her.

Without even thinking about the craziness of what he was doing, Tyson rushed into his bedroom, grabbed an overnight bag and quickly began throwing items into it. She hadn't said anything about him being an overnight guest, but she would soon find out that he had a few conditions of his own.

Before zipping up the overnight bag he opened the drawer to his nightstand, reached inside and grabbed a handful of condoms. He was about to close the drawer, but then stopped and grabbed some more. Hell, for this little inconvenience, he intended to make tonight worth his while.

Chapter 8

Hunter glanced around her bedroom. Several candles were lit and the fragrance of vanilla floated in the air. She had changed the linens and sprayed vanilla mist over the sheets and pillows for an extra touch.

How many times had she envisioned setting up a bedroom room like this for Carter only to have him make fun of her attempt? That was after he'd accused her of trying to burn the house down with the candles and spraying stuff that he was probably allergic to. Her ex hadn't had a romantic bone in his body. Even during those times when they were trying to have a baby, he refused to let her turn their drab-looking bedroom into a romantic hot spot.

Now she had her hot spot. It was an important component in her plan of seduction. She didn't intend to start bed-hopping with men, by any means, but hopefully after this one time with Tyson, she would have the courage to at least date other men and see where it led.

She had no desire to ever get married again, nor was she interested in engaging in a serious relationship. Occasional dating would suit her just fine. If she liked the man well enough, she saw no reason why they couldn't share an intimate night once in a while. Granted, she had to feel the man was worthy of sharing her bed.

Then what was up with Tyson Steele? Was he worthy?

She wasn't sure about that, but he did know the right buttons to push to arouse her. And there was that element of sexual chemistry between them. So he might as well be her first test. Mo was right. If she was going to declare her sexual independence then it might as well be with Tyson.

At that moment the doorbell sounded. If that was Tyson, he'd arrived sooner than she'd anticipated. She figured he would at least take some time to mull over her offer. Since it appeared that he hadn't, she took it as a strong indication of just how eager he was to have sex with her.

They would have this one night together. In the end she would declare her sexual independence as well as get him out of her system. And if what everyone claimed was true, she would experience her first orgasm in years. Hopefully the dreams would stop coming and she could get a good night's sleep without waking up the next day with an ache between her legs.

Leaving her bedroom, she headed for the door. Halfway there she paused to draw in a deep breath. There was no need to get cold feet now, she told herself. Although she and Tyson might have different ideas regarding how to go about getting what they wanted, she was certain they wanted the same thing. This was not the time to question her decision to seduce him. It would be a win-win situation for the both of them, she reminded herself. Tyson could then move on to the next woman and she could concentrate on building her company.

Hunter opened her front door and he stood there. She could only stare at him, taking in all six feet and more of him. Tyson had a way of making any woman's body snap to salacious attention whenever she saw him. Already the tips of her breasts were responding to his masculine form. Sexual hunger, the likes of which she experienced only in his company, was taking a greedy hold on her.

She saw his overnight bag. Did he honestly assume she would invite him to stay the night? If so, he would be sorely disappointed later when showed him the door. She moved aside. "It didn't take you long to get—"

That was as far as she got. Once inside, he shut the door, dropped the overnight bag to the floor and pulled her into his arms, slanting his mouth across hers.

Tyson hadn't meant to kiss her. This was her show and he'd intended to let her play it out however she chose. He had every intention of just being a willing participant. But when she'd opened that door and he'd gotten a glimpse of that dress again, he couldn't resist pulling her into his arms and kissing her like he'd wanted to do at his place but hadn't gotten the chance. Now he was getting his fill of her taste.

At least she hadn't tried breaking free of his kiss. In fact she was kissing him back with a hunger that nearly matched his own. He loved the way their tongues mated, how hers mingled with his. His heart was racing. He tried to recall the last time a woman did that to him, but couldn't.

Tyson was fully aware that being here with her was overriding common sense and overlooking good sound judgment. He knew better, yet he was refusing to heed those warnings that went off in his head on the drive over here. He had called himself all kinds of fool for chasing after a woman for a one-night stand.

He would deal with the craziness of that later, once he'd gotten her out of his system. But for now all he could do was accept that there was something about Hunter McKay that had him wanting sex, sex and more sex. But only with her.

Moments later, just like he'd been the one to initiate the kiss, he was the one to end it, drawing in a deep delicious breath that included a whiff of her scent. But he was in no hurry to release her. Instead he held her in his arms while he pressed a series of kisses around the curve of her mouth and the tip of her nose. Knowing if he didn't stop touching her now that he never would, he released her and took a step back. The separation almost killed him.

He looked over at her and saw her looking at him. A part of him wanted to read her thoughts, but he figured it was probably best if he didn't know them. She didn't seem upset or annoyed, just somewhat pensive. He'd learned a woman absorbed in her own thoughts was the worst kind because he had no idea what they were thinking...or planning.

Finally, she spoke. "Now that you've gotten that out of your system, will you let me be in charge from here on out?"

Was her assumption true? Had he gotten anything out of his system? He seriously doubted it. Instead of sharing that doubt with her, he shoved his hands into the pockets of his jeans. It was either that or pull her back into his arms.

Forcing that thought from his mind, he dwelled on what she'd asked him. She wanted him to relinquish his control to a woman. To her. Under normal circumstances he would never agree to something like that. But he'd reached the conclusion while racing from his condo to here that nothing about any of this was normal.

"So, Tyson, are you going to let me handle things or not?" she asked again when he evidently hadn't responded quickly enough.

She'd asked him to let her handle *things*. As far as he was concerned, *things* didn't necessarily include him, but he wouldn't tell her that just yet. He was curious to see what she had up her sleeves. If truth be told, sleeves be damned. What he was really interested in was what was up under her dress.

"I suppose I can let you handle things," he finally said.

She raised a brow. "You 'suppose'? Need I remind

you that the moment you walked through that door you entered my territory? You came to me."

He frowned. Did she have to rub it in? "And we both know why," he said. "So why are we still talking?"

She smiled calmly. "You're trying my patience."

He chuckled. "And you've been trying mine since that night we ran into each other at Notorious."

"Would you like to sit and talk a while?"

"No. I have nothing to say and that's not why I'm here."

"I know why you're here, but first I think we need to understand each other," she said.

"Meaning?"

"For starters, I don't know what's up with that bag. Since you aren't a doctor who makes house calls, I can only assume you think you're spending the night. Well, you aren't. You will leave when we're done."

When they were done? Did she assume they would only go one round? He intended to stay the night and take her again and again, well into the morning hours.

"We can discuss that later, Hunter." He figured after he had her once, she'd beg him for more.

"No, I think we need to discuss it now."

He simply stared at her for a moment and then nodded. "Fine. I'll go along with whatever you want," he said, telling her what she wanted to hear. Evidently he'd said the magic words, if the smile that spread across her lips was anything to go by. "I guess I just made your day," he said drily.

"Yes, and I plan to make your night, Tyson Steele."

* * *

Hunter felt in control and she intended to use it to her advantage. She'd never done anything like this before, but she was ready to set the stage for what she had in store for Tyson.

"Go sit on the sofa, Tyson, and get comfortable. Make yourself at home."

A smile touched the corners of his mouth. "At home I tend to walk around in the nude. Can I do it here?"

"No." The thought of him doing such a thing made her nipples harden even more. "Would you like something to drink?"

He shook his head as he moved toward her sofa. "I had wine at dinner. I'm good."

Hunter watched how he eased his body down on her sofa, and how the denim jeans stretched across his muscled thighs. She couldn't wait to actually see those thighs in the flesh. In her dreams she had kneeled between them and—

"Nice place."

She hoped he hadn't noticed the splash of color that had appeared on her cheeks, a result of where her thoughts had been. "Thanks. Not as roomy as yours but it suits me just fine."

He stretched his arms across the back of her sofa as he leaned back in a comfortable position. Doing so brought emphasis to his chest. She looked forward to removing his shirt and was itching to rub her hand against his hard chest and flat stomach. Then she would ease her hands lower to cup him, to feel the part of him that had played a vital role in her dreams.

She could feel more heat in her cheeks. For a woman who hadn't been sexually active in four years, and who hadn't even thought much about it, her mind was having a field day.

Deciding to set the mood, she flicked off the ceiling lights so the living room could be bathed in the soft glow of the two floor lamps. She glanced over and saw him watching her, and desire rippled down her spine. She joined him on the sofa, sitting beside him but not too close. She found the distance really didn't matter. Nothing could eliminate the manly heat emanating from him. Because of it, her skin felt noticeably warm through her dress.

"So, Tyson, how was your day?" She decided a neutral topic was a perfect way to break the ice. But with all the heat surrounding them she knew anything cool didn't have much chance of survival.

A slow, sexy smile spread across his lips. "I don't recall most of it. I slept for the past forty-eight hours, remember."

"Yes. You did mention that."

"Now I'm wide-awake, full of energy and horny as hell."

The man knew just the right words to say to make every hormone in her body sizzle. "Are you?"

"Yes."

"Sleep makes you horny?" She glanced down at his thighs and saw the huge erection bulging between them, pressing against his zipper.

"Only when you occupy my dreams."

His words surprised her and she glanced up and

stared into his face. Had he been dreaming about her like she'd been doing of him? "And what were we doing in your dreams?" she asked, as if she really didn't know. It made sense that when a man like Tyson had dreams they would be nothing but erotic.

"We were making love."

She arched a brow. "For forty-eight hours?"

He chuckled softly, as if remembering. "Yes. We had a lot of ground to cover. A lot of years to make up for. A lot of positions to try."

Imagining a few of those positions had her pulse pounding. "Did we?"

He gave her a sensuous grin. "Yes, we did."

Hunter released a heated breath as his words painted an erotic picture in her mind, making shivers rush up her spine. She held his gaze, felt the stimulating attraction between them. Her face lowered again to the area between his thighs. Was she imagining it or had his erection gotten larger? Thicker? Harder?

She glanced back up at him and saw his smile had widened, as if he'd read her thoughts. But there was no way he could have, she assured herself. He was holding her gaze and sensations began pricking her skin. She didn't have to wonder what the look in his eyes meant.

"Now I know your secret weapon for seduction, Tyson," she said.

"I didn't know I had one."

"You do."

"Then tell me what it is," he said and she didn't miss how he'd spread his legs so his thigh brushed her thigh, which wasn't covered by her short dress. The contact was stimulating and she was tempted to close her eyes and moan.

"It's your eyes," she said, staring into them. "You can literally seduce a woman without opening your mouth. All you have to do is level those green eyes on her."

"You think so?"

"Aren't you trying to seduce me?"

"No. We agreed that you would seduce me. The look you see in my eyes is nothing more than an indication of just how much I want you."

If he thought his words were getting to her, then he was right. Maybe it was time she let a few of hers get next to him.

"I've turned my bedroom into a romantic hot spot just for tonight," she said softly.

She saw the desire in his eyes deepen. "Did you?"

"Yes. I think you'll like it."

"A long as you're in there with me, there's no doubt that I will."

Hunter drew in a deep breath. "It's the first time I've ever done that." She wondered why she felt the need to mention that.

"Lucky me."

Yes, lucky you, she thought. The husky tone of his voice had her easing a little closer to him. It felt like the natural thing to do. And then she reached out and placed her hand on his thigh. Doing that felt natural, as well. The muscles in his thigh tightened beneath her fingers and she heard his sharp intake of breath. She couldn't help but be pleased with his response.

"What if I told you that I've dreamed of you, as

well, Tyson?" she whispered close to his ear. He smelled good. He smelled like a man.

"Would you like to compare notes?"

His question made hot and sharp desire claw at her. Comparing notes with him *would* be interesting. "That's not necessary. I have a few good ideas of my own."

"I was hoping you did."

Considering that this was Tyson Steele, who went through women quicker than he changed his socks, Hunter wondered if what she had planned would suffice. She was a novice and he was so damn experienced. But he had agreed to let her handle things and she would, in her own way.

She felt in control. Bold. Daring. And she intended to play out her fantasies. Who said only men were allowed to have them? There were a few she hadn't shared with anyone, not even Mo or Kat. She had tried sharing them with Carter, only to get laughed at. She had a feeling Tyson wouldn't find any of them amusing. Her heart skipped a beat at the thought that with this bad boy of Phoenix she could be a bad girl. Besides, it was only for one night.

Hunter slid her hand closer to his crotch, and as she slowly stroked him there, she heard his breath hitch.

When her nerve endings began feeling somewhat edgy and the area between her legs began tingling, she decided there was no reason to waste any more time. She stood up. "Umm, it's hot in here. I think I'm wearing too many clothes."

And then, while he watched, she began removing them.

Chapter 9

Tyson leaned forward in his seat, resting his forearms on his thighs and not taking his eyes off Hunter. If a strip show was part of her seduction then she could seduce him anytime or anyplace...including here, the place she called home. His objection to spending the night in her bed instead of his own lost some of its punch. The main thing on his mind right now was seeing her naked body. The body he had dreamed about every single night since their paths had crossed.

She had kicked off those killer heels and the first thing he noticed was that her toenails were painted a fiery red. He thought she had pretty feet. Sexy feet. Tyson had never been a toe kisser, but had to admit that seeing hers was giving him some new ideas.

And then she went for her dress, that very short

dress, and began easing it down those gorgeous legs. Slowly she exposed a black lace bra and then matching panties. Seeing Hunter stand before him in just her bra and panties, he felt a slow, sensuous stirring in the pit of his stomach that made his erection even harder.

And when she reached up and released the front clasp to her bra, he almost tumbled off the sofa. Her breasts weren't just beautiful. They were absolutely, positively perfect. The nipples were dark and already hard. His tongue moved around in his mouth, in anticipation of licking them. Just staring at the twin globes made him eager for the feel of them in his hands and pressed against his bare chest.

She had a small waist and a flat stomach, and her thighs were a lover's dream. So perfect, he could imagine his body being cradled inside them.

His gaze was drawn to her fingers as she placed them beneath the waistband of her panties. From their slight tremor, it appeared she was getting somewhat nervous as a result of his intense gaze. But it couldn't be helped. He didn't intend on missing a thing. His brothers were either breast or leg men, and although he appreciated both, he was a vagina man all the way. As far as he was concerned there was no part of a woman's body that he found more fascinating than her V. So, he couldn't help it when his gaze lowered to her center in anticipation.

"I see I have your attention, Tyson," she said in a husky breath.

"You had my attention the moment you stood up, Hunter."

"Did I?"

"I wouldn't lie to you."

He wondered if the pose she was standing in—her legs braced apart and her fingers tucked into the flimsy lace material—was deliberate on her part to make him crave her even more. "After I remove my panties it will be your turn to take everything off," she declared huskily.

"It will be my pleasure."

"No, Tyson. I'm going to make sure it's *my* pleasure."

He didn't have a problem with that because he knew any pleasures that came under this roof tonight would be shared by the both of them. Tyson shifted his body somewhat to ease some of the hardness behind the zipper of his jeans, as well as to get a closer eye view of the part of her she was about to unveil. She paused a minute and held his gaze. She had to know what she was doing. All this stalling was nothing short of pure torture for him.

"You're panting, Tyson."

Was he? It wouldn't surprise him if he was.

"I'm certain you've seen this part of a woman many times," she said in a sultry tone. "And I'm also sure if you've seen one you've seen them all."

Hardly, Tyson thought, trying to retain his sanity. He had seen this part of a woman many times, but it would be his first time seeing hers and for some reason the thought had him aching. What in the hell was this woman doing to him? Never in his life had he been this desperate to see a woman totally naked.

"Since you seem to have such a high degree of interest in this, would you like to finish undressing me?" she asked him.

He swallowed a deep lump in his throat. "You trust me to do that?" he asked.

She chuckled. "It's just a pair of panties, Tyson. All you have to do is take them off me. Besides, you're here on my turf, so no matter what happens from here on out, it's still my seduction and not yours."

Why she had a problem with getting seduced, he still wasn't sure. But at the moment, he didn't care. He had a feeling that tonight would be a night that he wouldn't forget in a long time. He intended to make it so.

"Well?"

"I'd love to." Tyson eased from the sofa to stand in front of her for a second, before kneeling down on his knees. He was now on eye level with the one part of her that he wanted most. His erection throbbed, begging for release. She was sexy as hell and the man in him appreciated everything about her...especially this.

Tyson leaned forward and pressed his face against the lace. He couldn't resist nuzzling her while drawing in deep breaths, needing to absorb her intimate fragrance through his nostrils.

"What are you doing?" she asked him in a choppy voice.

"Inhaling your scent." He figured that Hunter could pretend indifference all she wanted, but this intimate act had to be doing something to her. "I love your personal fragrance, Hunter." *Maybe too much*, he thought, but pushed that reflection to the back of his mind.

"Do you?"

"Can't you tell?" Leaning back on his haunches he slowly began easing the lace panties down her legs, exposing what had to be the most beautiful V any woman could possess. She was wrong. When you saw one you hadn't seen them all. He was convinced that just like a fingerprint, a woman's feminine mound, the very essence of her being, was an exclusive part of her.

And this was hers. It belonged to Hunter McKay and it was beautiful in all its natural setting. Some men were big on the shaved or waxed look, but he wasn't one of them. This was his preference.

When she stepped out of her panties and kicked them aside, he reached up and began caressing her thighs, loving the feel of her soft skin beneath his fingertips. Then he began stroking her stomach, thinking that even her belly button was beautiful. His tongue itched to lick her, but instead he used his index finger to draw circles around her V a few times before running his fingers through the beautiful curls covering it.

"Tyson…"

His name was spoken from her lips in a sensuous whisper. He lifted his head and met her gaze. He saw all the heat flaring in the dark depths staring back at him and understood the feeling. He was there, close to the edge, right along with her. "Yes?" he answered huskily, while his fingers continued to stroke between her legs. She was wet…just the way he liked.

"I——I need f-for you to take off your clothes," she said, barely getting the words out.

He figured that might be her need, but his tongue had a different need right now. "Can I get a lick first?"

The heat he saw in her eyes flared and his fingers

could feel her get wetter. "Just one?" she asked, holding tight to his gaze.

"Possibly two. Maybe three. I'll admit that I'm one greedy ass."

Color had come into her cheeks so he could only assume her ex either hadn't gone down on her too often, or not at all. What a damn shame. Well, he intended to make up for it.

"In that case," she finally said, "help yourself."

Filled with a need he didn't understand but one he was driven to accept, Tyson spread her thighs apart and used his fingers to open her before dipping his head. The moment his tongue captured her clit he moaned deep in his throat the same time she did. He licked once, twice, three times. And when he couldn't get enough her of delicious taste, he locked his mouth to her, held tight to her thighs and drove his tongue inside her as far as it could go. She'd told him to help himself, and he intended to do just that.

The Tyson Steele way.

Hunter felt her world spinning. Weak from the feel of Tyson's tongue thrusting deep inside her, she reached out to grab hold of his shoulders for support. Nothing, and she meant nothing, could have prepared her for what she was feeling. She had no idea that something like this could bring her so much pleasure. Oral sex was something Carter had frowned upon. More than once he'd said that a man's mouth was not meant to go between a woman's legs, and he claimed most men felt that way.

Evidently Tyson had a totally different opinion about

that, judging by the way he was working his tongue inside her. The man was a master at this, an undisputed pro. She arched her back to give him further access as every nerve ending in her body threatened to explode. She'd told Mo and Kat that she hadn't had an orgasm in so long she'd forgotten how it felt to have one. Tyson was rekindling her memory in one salacious way. If he didn't release her soon, she'd climax right in his mouth.

She tightened her grip on his shoulders and in a ragged voice said, "You got to stop, Tyson. I'm about to—"

Too late. She screamed at the same time spasms speared her body, detonating in an explosive orgasm and nearly shattering her to pieces. Instead of removing his mouth, Tyson drove his tongue even deeper inside her. The lusty sounds he made pushed her over the edge again. And he still wouldn't release her.

When the last of the spasms had left her body, he freed his mouth from her and eased back on his haunches to look up at her. She moaned at the sight of him licking his lips.

He eased to his feet and said, "Now I get to take off my clothes."

Tyson couldn't resist licking his lips again. Hunter's taste was simply incredible. He was convinced it was the most delicious flavor he'd ever tasted. He figured her taste was imprinted on his tongue and would remain there forever.

Forever. He went still. Surely he didn't think that. Forever was something he could never equate with any woman. All he was feeling at the moment was some exceptional brand of passion, one so remarkable it had temporarily affected his brain cells.

The only other excuse he could come up with to explain such crazy thoughts was that he'd relinquished control to her just by showing up here. He had allowed her to seduce him and wasn't sure doing so had been the right thing. It had been seduction this time, but what if she tried making him beg for it the next? Tyson inwardly cringed at the thought and knew giving her any type of empowerment again wouldn't be happening. He had a mind to leave right now. Walk out the door and not look back.

But there was no way he could do that. He wanted her way too much and didn't plan to go anywhere. So much for taking the upper hand and putting things in perspective, he thought. But then he looked at it in another way. It was about getting Hunter out of his system and getting from her what she had refused him eighteen years ago. After tonight she would be out of sight and out of mind.

He glanced over at her, saw her studying his mouth as if she couldn't believe what he'd just used it for. *Believe it*, he wanted to say. *In fact, I plan on using it again the same way before the night is over.*

Moments later her gaze shifted from his mouth to his eyes. She looked at him with an intensity that he felt in every part of his body. She'd accused him of using his eyes to seduce her, but whether she knew it or not, at that moment she was using hers to render him totally helpless. He felt a degree of passion he'd never felt before.

The chemistry surrounding them had heightened. He was aroused to a level that at any other time—and with any other woman—he would have considered unnerving. The fact that she was standing a few feet away from him completely naked, and that he'd just gotten a damn good taste of her, had to be the reason his erection was throbbing mercilessly behind his zipper.

Breaking eye contact, Tyson eased down on the sofa to remove his shoes and socks. He then stood and his hand went to the waistband of his pants—he knew she was watching his every move.

He unsnapped his jeans, began lowering the zipper and slowly slid the jeans down his legs before stepping out of them. He had stripped down to his briefs and could feel her gaze roaming over him. His body became more heated.

Tyson was tempted to return the favor and asked if she wanted to remove his last stitch of clothing, but couldn't. If she was to touch him, he would tumble her to the floor and take her then and there. So he slowly eased his briefs down his legs, noting how her eyes widened.

"You're huge," she gasped with wonder in her voice.

His lips curved in what he knew was an arrogant smile. "You're handling things and you can handle this," he assured her. "Trust me."

Hunter stared at Tyson, finding it difficult to breathe. He was standing barely three feet away, naked as the day he was born and proudly displaying an erection so huge she figured it would put every other man to shame. Her stomach began quivering just from looking at it. The thought of it inside her filled her with a need she'd never felt before.

But that wasn't the only part of him she found impressive. Tyson Steele was beautiful from the top of his head to the soles of his feet. The man was built. Perfectly. All muscle and not an ounce of fat anywhere. He was a true work of art with firm thighs, strong masculine legs, a muscular chest and broad shoulders. At some point before the night was over, she intended to make it her business to lick every inch of him.

The very thought of doing that caused a slow stirring to erupt in the pit of her stomach. When had she become this sensuous being who suddenly needed sex like she need to take another breath? And why had it taken Tyson to make her feel this way?

Her gaze met his and she was captured by the intensity of his green eyes. He moved to retrieve something from his overnight bag and she saw it was a condom packet. As he walked back to her, his stride was slow, masculine and sexy as hell. Just watching his approach made her weak in the knees. When he came to a stop directly in front of her, he shifted his gaze from her eyes to her chest. Specifically her breasts. Her nipples automatically hardened to tight buds.

Without saying a word he lowered his mouth and took a nipple between his lips. She couldn't do anything but moan at the sensations that suddenly rammed through her. The sounds he was making while feasting on her conveyed his enjoyment, and she reached out and placed her hands on both sides of his head to hold him there. Yes, right there.

A while later he released one nipple and immediately sought out the other, and she let out another deep moan. He'd already made her come twice from his mouth between her legs and now he threatened to make her explode a third time just from having her breast in his mouth.

"Tyson, w-we need to get t-to the bedroom," she said in a heated breath, while fighting to hold back yet another moan.

Before she could take her next breath, he swept her off her feet and into his arms. "Tell me where, so I can take you there."

Chapter 10

Tyson placed Hunter on the bed then took a step back, letting his gaze roam over her from head to toe. He doubted he'd ever seen a more perfect woman. Every inch of her was flawless. He'd taken a good look at her while she'd been standing naked in her living room. But there was just something about a woman stretched out in bed, waiting to be taken, that did something to him every time.

Especially with this woman.

His gaze moved around the room. She had referred to it as a romantic hot spot and he could see why. There were candles and throw pillows situated around the room, wineglasses, a bottle of wine chilling in an ice bucket and a tray of different cheeses on a small table near the bed. Soft music was playing and the bedcovers were turned back. The ambiance was one of romance and at that moment he was looking forward to a night of passion with her.

"This room looks wonderful, Hunter. You did a great job setting the mood."

"Did I?"

He heard the surprise in her tone and glanced at her. That's when he saw the brilliance of her smile and knew his compliment had pleased her greatly. That made him wonder. Had she done a similar setup for that ass she'd been married to and the man hadn't appreciated her effort?

"Yes, you did," he assured her. "You know how to take seduction to one hell of an amazing level. Hunter McKay, you can seduce me anytime." And at that moment, he truly meant it.

He appreciated that she still lay on top of the covers, where he'd placed her, and hadn't gotten beneath them. His gaze roamed all over every inch of her body. He would enjoy making love to her, touching her, licking her all over, tasting her again, and was driven by a desire to savor every minute of doing so. Just looking at her, thinking of everything he intended to do to her and how he would do it, made his erection harder.

But first he needed to prepare himself for her. While she watched, he sheathed himself with a condom. "You just brought one?" she asked him.

He glanced up at her and smiled. "No. I brought a few." He figured it was best not to admit to having an overnight bag full. He didn't want to scare her.

Then he moved forward. He kneeled on the bed and

slowly crawled toward her. He remembered that first night at Notorious, when he'd decided he would be the hunter and she his prey. Now he wasn't sure which one of them had truly been captured.

He went straight for her mouth, needing to kiss her. The kiss was meant to arouse her, but when she began responding, he was the one getting even more aroused. Their tongues mingled, tangled madly, mated hotly, and his hands began to move, cupping those same breasts he'd sucked on earlier, loving how they fit in his hands.

Moments later he released her mouth and his lips trailed a path down to her breasts, needing to taste them again. The nipples were hard and ready for his mouth and he devoured them with a greed he only had for her.

Not able to hold off any longer, he tore his mouth away from her breasts to move up over her body. He glanced down at her. She looked beautiful, the glow from the candles dancing across her features.

He braced himself on his elbows as he continued to stare down at her. And then he sucked in a deep breath when she deliberately pushed up her breasts to rub them against his chest, as if doing so had been her fantasy. The feel of her hard nipples brushing against his chest did something to him. From the look on her face it was doing something to her as well.

"You like that?" he asked her.

"Yes. What about you?"

He didn't have to think about his answer. The feel of her nipples teasing the hair on his chest felt damn good. "Yes, I like it. Umm, what do you think of this?"

He reached down and widened her legs before lowering his body to settle his chest between them. And then he began deliberately moving his body to stroke his chest hair against the curls covering her V. He could tell from the look in her eyes that she found what he was doing stimulating.

"I like this," she said in a breathless tone.

"So do I," he said, feeling her dampen his chest. "Now for the main attraction." He eased his body back up until his erection touched the entrance to her body.

He glanced down at her and smiled. "You seduced the hell out of me tonight, Hunter. I liked it."

And with that, he thrust into her.

Hunter moaned at the feel of Tyson filling her so completely. She could actually feel his erection get harder while sliding deep inside her. He began moving, going in and then withdrawing, establishing a sensuous rhythm that had her alternating between clawing his back and gripping the bedspread. His hips and thighs jackhammered with lightning speed and when she let out one moan, she was already working on the other.

Had four years of abstinence done this to her? Make her body hungry? Greedy? Needy? She knew deep down that the length of time she'd gone without sex had nothing to do with it. It was Tyson and what he was doing to her. How he was making her feel. Whoever started the rumor that a woman hadn't truly been made love to unless it was by a Steele knew exactly what she was talking about.

Being here with Tyson was what true lovemaking was all about. The giving and sharing of pleasure was so profound she could feel it in her bones. Neither was dominant over the other; rather, they were equals. She couldn't help but let herself go and was caught up in the pounding of his body into hers.

When he threw his head back and let out a voracious growl it seemed the cords in his neck would pop. As if on cue her body detonated with his and sparks of passion began flying everywhere, igniting inside her a maelstrom of need that only Tyson could satisfy.

He bucked and then plunged downward at the same time her hips automatically lifted to receive him. He went deeper than before and she could feel every inch of him inside her.

She screamed at the same time he shouted her name while thrusting into her several more times as if he couldn't get enough. She held him tight and continued to move her body with his when she felt another delicious shiver race down her spine. And then she was screaming again, and from the way he was thrusting into her body she knew he'd had another orgasm, as well.

"Hunter…"

He said her name moments before collapsing onto her. A short while later he held up his head, eased up toward her lips and without saying anything, he kissed her again, this time with a tenderness that had a thick lump forming in her throat.

When he released her mouth she smiled up at him and he smiled back. Her heart began fluttering deep in her chest at the realization that she was the one responsible for his smile.

* * *

Hours later, Tyson eased his body off Hunter to lie beside her, flat on his back. Seeing that she had dozed off to sleep, he let out a whoosh of heated breath. How many rounds had this been so far? Five?

The two of them were mating like damn rabbits, and he still hadn't gotten enough of her. Every part of his body was sizzling for more. In the bedroom Hunter had been one of the most giving and one of the most passionate of any women he'd ever slept with, and considering his history with women that said a lot. She had totally overwhelmed him and no woman should have the ability to do that.

He would have frowned at the thought, but he couldn't help but smile as he recalled the look on her face when, after their first time, he'd dumped a handful of condoms on the table by the bed. He'd told her there was plenty more where those came from, and her eyes had gotten as big as saucers and her mouth had dropped open. "Do you really expect to use all of them?" she'd asked. Well, it was a moot point now, he thought as he looked at the handful of empty packages.

They had worked up an appetite after round three and sat naked in bed while drinking wine and eating an assortment of cheeses. They used that time to talk. He brought her up-to-date on former classmates and what they were doing now. He told her about his brother Jonas and his marriage to Nikki, Eli's marriage to Stacey and how his parents had stepped into the role of grandparents to Galen's twins with ease.

In turn, she told him about this house she'd designed

a few years ago for a well-known NBA player, and how she'd taken a Mediterranean cruise last year with some college friends. He'd noted she hadn't brought up anything about her ex and he was glad she hadn't.

Afterward, they had made love a couple more times and each had been just as intense and passionate as the other times had been. He discovered there was more passion in Hunter's pinky finger than some women had in their entire bodies. He loved the way she responded to his kisses, his touch and even the naughty, explicit words he would whisper in her ear to let her know just what he intended to do to her and how.

Jeez. When had he wanted a woman so badly, that even now he felt a surge of hot energy consume his groin? Just thinking about her, he was hard and longed to slide his erection back inside her to start round six. But he refused to wake her up. She needed her rest.

And, dammit, he needed to think.

Now was the time for logic to set in. Instead of waiting for her to wake up so he could make love to her again, he should be putting on his clothes and hauling ass, not caring if their paths ever crossed again. But logic wasn't working in his favor tonight. He didn't want to put on his clothes, and leaving was the last thing on his mind.

Why?

The question echoed in his head in the quiet room. He had gotten what she'd refused to give him eighteen years ago and he should be feeling like a score had been settled. The one who'd gotten away was now had. So why wasn't he pounding his chest with his fist, proud of himself, pleased with the way the night had turned out? Oh, he was pleased with the way the night had turned out, but it had nothing to do with him settling an old score. Far from it.

For the first time in his life he had truly enjoyed making love to a woman—every single aspect of it. The touching, tasting and thrusting had been off the charts. Mind-boggling. Super awesome. And the Mark of Tyson wasn't just on her neck, but was probably on every single part of her body. But he didn't see the mark as a sign of conquest. In his mind it had become a sign of possession.

Possession? Tyson rubbed his hand down his face as he tried to figure out how in the hell he could fix his mind to even think that way. He was a die-hard bachelor who enjoyed too many women to get hung up on just one. So there had to be a reason why he was having these possessive feelings toward Hunter.

One reason could be that for the first time in his life a woman had been a challenge. That had to be it. Other women made things easy for him, and the novelty of Hunter giving him a hard time had him thinking crazy thoughts. All it would take to clear his mind would be a few more rounds of sex with her to be assured that she was out of his system. A good night's sleep in her bed wouldn't hurt, either. When he woke up in the morning there was no doubt in his mind he would be thinking straight. When he left here it would be business as usual.

But still…

For some reason he was driven to mentally replay every single thing that had happened to him since running into Hunter more than two weeks ago. One thing stood out: he hadn't slept with another woman since then. Given his track record, that was odd. No, it was downright strange. He'd gotten plenty of calls, even one from that cute little ER nurse who was helping out temporarily in Cardio. Her name was Macy Phillips and she was on his "to do" list. So why hadn't he done her? What was he waiting for? She was definitely willing. And what about Kristen Fulbright, Nancy Heartwood and Candace Lane? Why had he begun thinking of them as history?

Hunter stirred beside him in bed and he glanced over at her just as her eyes flitted open. At that moment he thought the same thing that he had when he'd seen her that night in Notorious. She was beautiful. She stared back at him with a sleepy look in her eyes. For a minute it was as if she was trying to recall why he was in her bed.

"Do I need to remind you?" he asked, seeing her dilemma and leaning over to kiss her on the lips.

She drew in a deep breath and shook her head. "No, I remember now. What time is it?" she asked as she yawned and pulled herself up in bed. The sheet covering her breast slid down and she quickly jerked it back up. *Seriously, Hunter, don't get all modest on me now when last night those nipples had seemed like a permanent fixture in my mouth.*

Instead of calling her out on it, he glanced over at the digital clock on her nightstand. "It's three in the morning."

She yawned again. "Sorry, I passed out on you."

"That's fine. You definitely needed your rest." He saw the color that flashed across her cheeks. "You're embarrassed?"

She shrugged. "Shouldn't I be? I screamed around ten times tonight. I can just what imagine what my neighbors think."

"It was twelve."

She lifted a brow. "Excuse me?"

"You screamed twelve times. Not ten. And your neighbors probably thought you were having a hell of a good time and wished it was them."

The color in her cheeks deepened. "Yes, well, I was having a good time. But all good things must come to an end, including your visit to my bed."

Tyson frowned. "You're kicking me out?"

"I told you that you weren't spending the night."

Yes, she had. "But that was before the twelve screams."

She actually had the gall to look confused. "What does that have to do with anything?"

Tyson figured if she had to ask then maybe he needed to make sure she screamed twelve more times. She had seduced him earlier, so maybe it was his time to seduce her. Instead of answering her question, he asked one of his own. "Do I get a kiss for the road, since this will be our last time together like this?"

She seemed to ponder his question for a second and then nodded. "Sure. Why not? Kiss me and then I'll walk you to the door."

Tyson smiled, thinking that by the time he finished kissing her she wouldn't be walking him anywhere.

She leaned toward him, evidently expecting a peck on the lips. He leaned in as well and started off with just a light peck, but then he slid his tongue into her mouth at the same time his hand slid under the covers to settle beneath her legs.

Tyson was prepared for her reaction and deepened the kiss. He began dueling with her tongue, deliberately inflicting all kinds of sensual torment, while at the same time his fingers did the same. He loved touching her this way. She was such a passionate woman and so damn hot.

He heard the groan in her throat but she didn't pull back from his kiss. Nor did she resist moments later when he eased her down on her back and continued to kiss her, thoroughly, deeply and possessively.

Possessively...

There was that word again. Why was it determined to invade his mind when it came to Hunter? Dismissing the question since he didn't have an answer, he turned his full concentration on the seduction of Hunter McKay. His desire revved up a notch when she returned his kiss as provocatively as he was giving it. When he felt his fingers get damp from the wetness between her legs, he knew what was next.

Round six.

He pulled back from the kiss to stare down at her and saw deep-seated desire etched in her eyes. She was aroused and so was he. He leaned in and whispered against her moist lips. "I want you. Say you want me again, too, Hunter."

Chapter 11

Tyson saw the battle taking place in the eyes staring back at him. Common sense versus intense desire. He recognized it because of a similar encounter with his own emotions earlier. He still hadn't figured out what was going on with him. The only thing he knew for certain was what he'd just told Hunter. He wanted her again.

"Say it," he whispered, brushing a kiss across her forehead. "Say you want me again, too." He tried to keep the urgency out of his voice, the hunger and need. But it couldn't be helped. The bottom line was that he needed to make love to her again as much as he needed to breathe.

She hesitated a minute longer, then said, "I want you again, too, Tyson."

Tyson released the breath he'd been holding and moved aside and made quick work of putting on another condom. In no time he was back, easing in place between her legs. He leaned in and captured her mouth at the same time he slid his hard erection inside her.

Once he was deeply embedded in her, he began moving, gently at first, one long stroke after another. But when he felt her nails dig deep into his back at the same time she rolled her hips beneath him, he picked up the pace and began pounding into her, hard and fast. He broke off the kiss and continued to thrust hard, over and over again. Grazing his jaw against her ear, he growled low in his throat. "Come for me, baby."

No sooner had he made the request than her body bucked in a bow beneath him and she screamed his name. "Tyson!"

But she didn't slow down. The spasms kept coming and she continued moving frantically beneath him, keeping up with the sensuous rhythm he'd established. Tyson decided that if she wanted a multiple orgasm this round then that's what he would give her. He sank deeper and deeper inside her while thrusting harder and harder.

His stomach clenched with need every time it touched hers and the hairs on his chest stirred to life whenever they came in contact with the hard nipples of her breasts. She tightened her legs around him and screamed his name at the same time he growled hers.

Fireworks seemed to go off inside Tyson's head. His entire body ignited into one hell of a gigantic explosion. He drew in a deep breath, thinking never had an orgasm felt so good. So perfect. The impact had his entire body quivering. Leaning down, he captured Hunter's mouth in a long, drugging kiss before easing off her to lie on his side.

Tyson pulled Hunter into his arms, entwining his legs with hers, still needing the connection. From the sound of her even breathing, he knew she had drifted back to sleep and he held her closer. Glancing down, he studied her features. She was a woman who didn't go out of her way to be sexy, yet she was sexy anyway. A woman who claimed she'd never seduced a man, but she had seduced the hell out of him. A woman who'd turned her bedroom into a romantic hot spot to set the mood for seduction. And a woman who had refused his advances until she'd gotten ready to accept them.

His brain felt as if it had short-circuited and he still didn't know why. So instead of getting more confused than he already was, he followed Hunter's lead and closed his eyes to join her in sleep.

As sunlight filtered through the window in her bedroom, Hunter slowly came awake. The even breathing close to her ear let her know she wasn't alone. She hadn't meant for Tyson to spend the night and had been pretty adamant that he didn't. All it had taken was a kiss, followed by another and topped with the best lovemaking she had ever experienced in her life to make her change her mind. Although she hadn't given Tyson the okay to stay, he had known. Why wouldn't he, when all he'd had to do was slide his hands between her legs or his tongue in her mouth and she became putty in his hands?

Probably just like all those other women.

She closed her eyes, not wanting to dwell on that thought now. But she knew she had to. She had no regrets about last night. Far from it. Tyson had opened her eyes to a lot of things, such as just how much of an ass Carter had been to deny her the very things she needed, not only as a wife but also as a woman.

She thought how she hadn't experienced an orgasm in four years, even longer if she was to count the times she'd shared Carter's bed and hadn't been fulfilled. Thanks to Tyson, she'd gotten more in one night than she'd had in all her years of marriage. She didn't want to think how many times she had screamed and wouldn't be surprised if her throat was sore this morning. So regardless of anything else, she appreciated Tyson for reminding her what it felt like to be a woman again. And what it felt like to have needs and have those needs satisfied to the fullest.

Not only had he given her a chance to seduce him, but he'd also agreed that she could to do it the way she wanted. Even after she'd told him she had never seduced a man before. Yet he had allowed her to take control, to "handle things," even when he hadn't fully understood her need to do so. He had no idea that last night restored her confidence in herself as a woman. It was the confidence Carter had painstakingly stripped from her.

However, upon waking up this morning she was faced with the realization that all good things must come to an end. After today, Tyson would go his way and she would go hers. In a day or two she would only be a fleeting memory to him, if that. At least she could say she never shared Tyson Steele's bed. He'd shared hers.

"You're awake."

Before she could react to his words, Tyson surprised her by drawing her even closer into the curve of his warm body. It had been a while since she'd awakened with a man in her bed, especially one who liked to snuggle and hold her through the night. Even when she and Carter had slept together, he had stayed in his corner of the bed and she'd stayed in hers. And those times when they did have sex, afterward they returned to those corners. It had never bothered her before because she'd gotten used to it. But spending one single night with Tyson was a stark reminder of what she'd put up with in her marriage.

Hunter tilted her head to look at Tyson and wished she hadn't. He had that early morning look—sleepy eyes with dark stubble along his chin and jaw—that begged for her touch. She was tempted to reach out and run her fingers along his chin to feel it for herself. She was convinced no man should look this sexy in the morning.

Finally, she responded to him. "Yes, I'm awake."

"Good. Take a shower with me before I leave."

Why did she get the feeling he seemed rather anxious to leave? And he wanted them to shower together? She honestly didn't think that was a good idea and was about to tell him so when he added, "Just one last thing we can do together."

He'd practically said the same thing about that kiss

last night. Only problem was one thing had led to another and then another. She could see taking a shower with him that lasted for hours. She'd discovered Tyson could be very creative when it came to sex and could just imagine some of his artistic ideas for her in the bathroom.

When she hesitated he nudged her. "Are you going to deny me the chance for you to wash my back?"

She couldn't help but chuckle. "Or deny you the chance to wash mine?" she countered.

"Umm, I have no problem washing your back...or any other part of you that you'd like me to give attention to."

Yes, she bet he wouldn't have a problem with it. "I think you gave enough attention to my body parts last night. I'll be surprised if I'm able to walk today."

"Sorry about that."

She waved off his words. "Don't apologize. I needed last night. Screams and all. Trust me."

He shifted to stare into her eyes. "Why?"

He didn't need to know, she thought. The less he knew about her needs, the better. "Doesn't matter. And I'll pass on sharing that shower with you. I'm not ready to get up yet."

"You sure?"

"Positive."

He stared at her for a second and then without saying anything else, he eased away from her, got out of the bed and headed out of the bedroom. "The bathroom is that way," she said to him, trying not to notice his nakedness. He had no shame walking around naked and she had no shame getting an eyeful. He had a beautiful body, one any woman would appreciate.

"I know. I need to grab my overnight bag from the living room."

She nodded, remembering the infamous bag. The one containing all those condoms they'd nearly gone through last night.

It took him only a minute to get the bag and she watched when he walked back through the bedroom and headed for the bathroom. He stopped and glanced over at her. "You're sure you don't want to join me?"

No, she wasn't sure, but she knew it would be for the best. Too much of Tyson could become addictive. "Yes, I'm sure."

Flashing a sexy smile, one that caused her pulse to race, he entered the bathroom and closed the door behind him.

Hunter shifted in the bed when she heard the sound of the shower. She glanced around the room. The candles had burned down but the fragrance of vanilla lingered in the air, along with that of sex. She felt a tingling sensation in her stomach at the memories of their lovemaking.

Hunter felt sore between her legs but the soreness would be a reminder of all the pleasure Tyson had given her. He had made back-to-back love to her, allowing her the chance to take naps in between. He had licked her all over and she didn't have to look down at herself to know he'd probably left passion marks all over her body. Hopefully by Monday they would have faded away. At least she wouldn't have to see anyone over the weekend. Her parents had gone to a motorcycle race, and her brother and his family had taken off to Disneyland.

She would lie around and recover from Tyson's love-making, although she knew it would take more than a weekend for her to do that. He had awakened desires in her that she hadn't known existed. No wonder he was in such high demand with women.

Deciding to cover her nakedness, she reached out and pulled open the drawer to the nightstand, where she kept her oversized T-shirts. Sliding one over her head, she didn't miss the passion marks on her chest, stomach and thighs. She figured she'd find the majority of them between her legs. His mouth seemed to particularly like that area of her body.

Hunter glanced over at the closed bathroom door, tempted to go join Tyson in the shower. She knew she wasn't thinking with her head, but with overactive hormones. The only good thing was that he was now out of her system, and she was sure she was out of his.

"I'm ready to leave."

She twisted around in bed. She hadn't heard Tyson come out of the bathroom, but there he was, standing in the middle of the room, fully dressed in a pair of khakis and a polo shirt. He'd shaved but she much preferred the rugged look on him. Still, he looked good.

"I'll walk you to the door." She eased out of bed and winced, feeling a definite soreness between her legs. She grabbed her bathrobe off the chair and put it on.

"You okay?" he asked, quickly crossing the room to her with a concerned look on his face.

"Yes, I'm fine. I just need to soak in a bath today for a while."

"Do you want me to run your bathwater before I go?"

She thought it was kind for him to offer. "No, that's not necessary, Tyson. I can manage."

He searched her face. "You sure?"

"Yes, I'm sure. Don't worry about me. I'll be fine." But even as Hunter said the words, a part of her wondered if she truly would be. Unknowingly, Tyson had given her something last night that no other man had given her. A chance to be herself. To live out her fantasies. To be the sensuous and passionate woman she'd always suspected she was.

Tyson nodded and for a long moment he stood there not saying anything and just looking at her, and she could feel his stare as if it was a heated caress. Then when she was about to ask him if there was something wrong, he finally said in a deep husky voice, "I don't want you to walk me to the door, Hunter."

She arched a brow. "Why?"

"Because I want you to get back in bed. That's the memory I want to leave here with. You in that bed. Your bed. Where we spent most of the night."

She didn't understand his request. "Why?"

A seriousness she'd never seen before touched his features. "I just do. Last night was special for me." He paused a moment and then said, "And about those house plans. When I get a chance to look over them I will. After I do, I'll get back to you."

She shrugged. "You don't really have to do that. We

both know the real reason you hired me to draw up those plans."

He didn't deny it. In fact he didn't say anything for a long moment and then he leaned down and brushed his lips across hers. She figured the kiss was supposed to be short and sweet. However, the moment their lips touched, he pulled her into his arm and went after her mouth with the greed she'd grown accustomed to.

Resisting never entered her mind. Instead she returned the kiss in the same way she figured he was accustomed to her doing as well. The intensity of his tongue mating with hers nearly brought her to her knees. She moaned in pleasure not only from the kiss, but also from the feel of his masculine strength. And although she should have preferred otherwise, she liked the feel of his hard, engorged erection cradled intimately at the juncture of her thighs. It wouldn't take much to tumble back in bed and take him with her. There was no doubt in her mind if that was to happen she would eventually let out more screams.

But Tyson suddenly broke off the kiss.

He straightened and then gently brushed his knuckles across her cheek. "Go ahead and get back in the bed, Hunter."

She nodded and removed her robe. For a quick second she was tempted to remove her T-shirt as well. However, she refused to give in to temptation. The last thing she wanted was to tempt him to stay and make love to her again. They were doing the right thing by parting this way. He was who he was and she was who she was. Besides, last night had only been about sex, so there was no need to get all emotional.

She tossed her robe on the chair and slid beneath the covers. Stretching out in bed she gazed up at him. "Goodbye, Tyson."

He stared at her for a long moment before finally speaking. "Goodbye, Hunter." And with his overnight bag clutched in his hand he walked out of the bedroom.

Hunter didn't release her breath until she heard her front door open and then close behind him.

Chapter 12

"So, what's been going on with you, Tyson?"

Tyson glanced over at his brother Galen. He had stopped by to see how Brittany and the twins were doing, as well as to see how his laid-back older brother was faring. It seemed Galen had everything under control and had accepted his role as father to twins pretty easily. Almost as easily as he'd stepped into his role as husband.

To this day it still confused the hell out of Tyson. Of the six of them, Galen had been the most notorious womanizer. His reputation had extended from Phoenix all the way to the Carolinas, specifically Charlotte, North Carolina, where their Steele cousins lived. Galen was the last person Tyson thought would settle down with one woman. Yet now he was a husband and a father. Tyson shook his head. And had he heard Brittany right at dinner tonight when she mentioned them buying a van? Galen was known for his love of sports cars and as a collector of muscle cars. A van was the last vehicle Tyson would have thought his brother would be caught driving.

Deciding to answer Galen's question, he said, "Nothing's been going on with me but the usual. I've been pretty busy at the hospital." But not too busy to think about Hunter McKay, Tyson thought.

This time last week he'd been inside her. It was hard to believe a full week had passed. He thought of her often. Too damn much, in fact. The days weren't so bad, since like he told Galen he was pretty busy at the hospital. But it was at night, mainly when he went to bed, when he mostly thought about her. Not making love to her in his bed had turned out to be a good thing, otherwise he would never get any sleep.

But still…he had made love to her and that was the crux of his problem. They had shared passion, passion and more passion. And now he couldn't get all that passion out of his mind. He would get an erection just remembering their times together. And what was even worse, it seemed his desire for other women had abandoned him. Women called but he didn't call them back. How crazy was that?

"It's Friday night and you're off work," Galen pointed out. "Why aren't you hanging out at Notorious? That's usually your mode of entertainment on the weekends."

He didn't need his brother to remind him of that.

"Would you believe me if I told you I'm getting bored with the place?"

Galen stretched his legs out in front of him. "Not unless there's a reason. Scoping out the women there used to be your favorite pastime."

Tyson was tempted to remind Galen that Notorious used to be Galen's favorite hangout for that same reason before his Brittany days.

"Is there a reason, Tyson?"

Tyson shrugged. "No reason."

It got quiet and that didn't bode well for Tyson. He knew Galen. He was trying to figure out things that weren't his business. Just because he was the oldest, Galen thought he had a right to know everything about what his five brothers were doing. That assumption might have had some merit when they were kids, but now he, Eli, Jonas, Mercury and Gannon were adults and didn't need their big brother looking over their shoulders.

"What's her name?"

Tyson frowned. "Whose name?"

"The woman who left her mark on you."

Tyson almost chuckled at that. Especially when he recalled all the marks he'd left on Hunter. "No woman left her mark on me, Galen. You're imagining things."

"Am I?"

To be honest, Tyson wasn't sure. He still dreamed of Hunter and thought about her all the time. It was quite evident to him that their tumble between the sheets hadn't worked her out of his system. That annoyed the hell out of him.

"Did I tell you how I met Brittany?"

"Yes," Tyson answered, taking a sip of his wine. "The two of you met for a brief while in New York when we were there for Donovan's wedding." Donovan Steele was their cousin who'd gotten married several years ago. If everyone thought Galen falling in love was a shocker, then Donovan doing so was an even bigger one.

"True, that's when we first met. We ran into each other again six months later here in Phoenix at the auction house. To make a long story short, she had something I wanted and I had something she wanted."

Tyson nodded. "And what did you have that she wanted?"

"The title to the house she's now turned into a school."

"And what did she have that you wanted?"

"Sex."

Tyson nearly choked on his drink. And then he quickly glanced around for his sister-in-law, hoping she hadn't heard what his brother just said.

Galen smiled. "Relax. Brittany went upstairs to put Ethan and Elyse to bed. But even had she heard me, she would have backed up my story, because it's the truth."

Tyson stared at his brother. "And you're telling me this why?"

"Because I know you, Tyson. I might not know all the particulars about what's going on with you—especially why you dropped by here tonight instead of going to Notorious, where there're a slew of women just waiting for you to make an appearance. For you to deny yourself a chance to take a woman home to warm your bed can only mean one thing."

"What?"

"There's some woman you've fallen for."

Tyson frowned. "I haven't fallen for her. Not exactly. Let's just say she left a lasting impression on me."

Galen chuckled. "In other words, she was good in bed. Almost too good to be true. And you're wondering if it was great sex or something else."

Tyson's frown deepened. Was that what he was really wondering? No, he assured himself. It wasn't anything other than great sex. His problem was that he wanted more of that great sex, which meant he wanted more of Hunter. One night hadn't been enough. "You're getting carried away, Galen. It's not that serious."

"Isn't it?"

"No."

"You sure?"

He hesitated a minute, then said, "Yes. I'm sure."

"I hope you're right. Take it from a man who thought there couldn't possibly be a woman out there I'd want forever. If there's that possibility, then you owe it to yourself to find out."

"So how was your night with Tyson?" Kat asked.

"Did he remind you just how great having an orgasm can be?" Mo queried.

Hunter figured the questions would come sooner or later. In a way she was surprised they hadn't come earlier. After all, it had been a week. She couldn't believe it was Friday already. This time last week she and Tyson were engaging in what had turned into a sex marathon. She no longer had dreams to contend with. Now she had full-fledged memories, which she discovered was even worse. Now she knew how it felt to be touched by a man, tasted by a man, and all she had to do was close her eyes to remember those hard thrusts into her body.

"Well, if you're not going to tell us, then…"

Hunter rolled her eyes. "I have no problem telling you what you want to know, since it was one and done. Yes, Kat, I went out with Tyson. We had dinner at his place and later we went to mine."

Kat arched a brow. "Why?"

Hunter took a sip of her tea before continuing. "Because I knew how the night would end, and I refused to be seduced by him and share a bed that a zillion other women had shared. I told him I would be the one doing the seducing and it had to be done at my place. In my bed."

Both women stared at her with something akin to amazement on their faces. "And he actually went along with it?" Mo asked.

"Yes."

Kat and Mo stared at each other for a minute, and then they stared back at her. Kat shook her head. "I can't imagine a Steele running behind a woman."

"He didn't run behind me, Kat. He merely came to my house to be seduced."

"Okay, forget the seduction part for now," Mo said. "Did you get the big *O* at least once?"

Hunter thought it would serve no purpose confessing just how many times she had gotten it. Whenever she thought about it, she found the entire experience almost too overwhelming. Tyson had the ability to make her come with his mouth on her breasts, licking around her navel, between her legs... She shifted in her seat just thinking about it. But all she said was "Yes."

"And was it worth all the trouble?" Mo asked.

Hunter couldn't help but smile at the memory. "Definitely. I can't speak for the other Steeles, but I can say the rumors about Tyson are true."

"Hot damn," Kat said, grinning.

"This calls for a toast," Mo added. "Your dry days are over and we have Tyson Steele to thank."

"Whatever," she said, deciding it was time to change the subject. Especially since talking about Tyson was making her think of him, wonder what he was doing, who he was with.

"Do you think the two of you will get together again?"

"No," Hunter said, responding quickly to Kat's question. "There was a lot of sexual chemistry between us and we needed to work it out of our system."

"Did you?" Kat asked.

"Did I what?"

"Get Tyson Steele out of your system?"

"Yes."

Mo didn't look convinced. "Are you saying that you haven't thought of Tyson Steele—not once—since that night? That you don't dream of the two of you reliving memories of last Friday night?"

Hunter glanced around the restaurant, hoping Mo's voice hadn't carried. "I'm not saying anything."

"Umm," both Mo and Kat said simultaneously.

Hunter frowned. "And what do you guys mean by *umm*?"

Mo smiled sweetly. "Trust me. You'll find out soon enough."

Tyson entered his home and glanced around. This was a Friday night and he was away from the hospital, yet he would be going to bed alone. It was so unlike him. And he'd been acting strangely in other ways, as well. In fact, lately he had begun finding Macy Phillips's phone calls so annoying that he had removed her from his "to do" list.

Had he somehow been turned off from beautiful, sexy women? He sucked in a deep breath, knowing that wasn't true. If given the chance, he would do Hunter McKay again in a heartbeat. Even more times than he'd done her last Friday night.

He threw his car keys on the table as he thought about what Galen had said. Sometimes his older brother talked pure nonsense, but tonight Tyson couldn't help wondering if perhaps he should heed his brother's words. Should he find out if the reason he couldn't get Hunter out of his mind was because of the great sex or something else?

He pulled his phone out of his back pocket and searched his contact list for her phone number. He was a second from calling her when he regained his senses. He repocketed the phone and went into his bedroom. He would get a good night's sleep, convinced that when he woke up in the morning, his outlook on things would be different. He forced a smile. He'd even give one of the women still on his "to do" list a call.

Chapter 13

"Honestly, Mom, skateboarding?"

Hunter had rushed to the hospital after getting a call from the ER nurse that her mother had been brought to the emergency room by ambulance due to an accident on a skateboard. She hadn't known what to expect and gave a sigh of relief upon discovering there were no broken bones, just scrapes and bruises.

"I wore a helmet and knee pads, Hunter," her mother said, seemingly somewhat aggravated over all the fuss being made over her.

"And it was a good thing you did, Mrs. McKay," the ER doctor said, shaking his head. "Your injuries could have been a lot worse. You'll be sore for a couple of days, but the X-rays don't show anything broken."

"Oh, I could have told you that," Ingrid McKay said

matter-of-factly. "In fact I tried to tell you, but you wouldn't listen," she said, scolding the doctor.

"Just following procedures," the doctor said, writing information in the chart he held in his hand. "You took a nasty fall. I'm writing a prescription for any pain you might start to feel later. And I suggest you stay off the skateboard for a while."

"Whatever," her mother grumbled under her breath.

Hunter rolled her eyes, hoping her mother took the doctor's advice. "Where's Dad?"

"Today was his golf day, so I had that nice nurse call you instead of Bernie. I didn't want to upset him. And I sure wasn't going to call Bernie Junior."

Of course you wouldn't, Hunter thought. Her brother would have read their mother the riot act. Now she understood his concerns about their parents' risky playtime activities. "Can you walk out to my car or do you want me to have the nurse get you a wheelchair?" she asked.

"Why would I need a wheelchair? I can walk."

"Just asking, Mom."

She was leading her mother toward the exit door when a deep, husky voice stopped her. "Hunter?"

Hunter didn't have to turn to know who the voice belonged to. The stirrings that suddenly went off in the pit of her stomach were a dead giveaway.

She turned around and before she could regain her composure enough to answer, her mother exclaimed, "Hey, aren't you one of those Steele boys?"

Hunter fought back a smile. The male standing before them was definitely no boy. She knew for a fact he was all man. Her pulse rate escalated when she recalled just how she knew that. It had been twelve days since she'd seen Tyson last. Twelve days. Not that she was counting. He looked good, even wearing scrubs.

She studied his features, the ones that still dominated her dreams every night. Her gaze latched on to his mouth, a mouth that had sent her over the edge so many times. And as she looked at him she saw the corners of his mouth hitch up in a smile at her mother's question.

"Yes, ma'am, I am," he said respectfully, extending his hand out to her mother. "I'm Tyson Steele."

Ingrid accepted Tyson's hand. "Those green eyes gave you away." She peered over her glasses to study the name tag on his jacket. "So you're a doctor?"

"Yes, I'm a heart surgeon. Someone came through ER needing my services." Tyson's gaze left Ingrid to return to Hunter. "Is everything okay?"

She nodded, not sure she could speak at that moment. Then she found her voice. "Yes, everything is okay. Mom took a fall on a skateboard. It could have been worse."

Tyson lifted an amused brow. "A skateboard?"

"Yes. Hopefully it was her first and last time trying one out."

"Don't count on it," Ingrid muttered under her breath. Before Hunter could give her mother a scolding retort, Ingrid spoke up. "I recall when the two of you attended the same high school."

"Yes, we did," Tyson said, nodding.

Hunter hoped that was all her mother remembered. The last thing she needed was her mother bringing up the short time she and Tyson had dated. "Well, we better get going," she said. "I want to get by the pharmacy to pick up Mom's prescription."

"All right," Tyson said, but he didn't move away. He held her gaze.

The sexual chemistry. The physical attraction. The desire. They were still there. She felt it and from the look in his eyes she knew that he felt it, too. Hadn't they worked all that out of their systems that night at her place?

Evidently they weren't the only ones feeling it, because at that moment Ingrid cleared her throat. When they both glanced over at her, Ingrid asked Tyson, "Are you the one who got expelled from high school for being caught under the bleachers with the principal's daughter?"

"Mom!"

Ingrid shrugged. "Just asking."

Tyson chuckled. "No, that was my brother Galen."

Hunter figured she needed to get her mother out of there before she remembered something else that was best forgotten.

She wasn't quick enough and Ingrid asked, "What about church?"

Tyson lifted a brow. "What about it?"

Ingrid had no problem telling him. "I see your parents on Sundays but I don't recall seeing you and your brothers."

Tyson grinned at her mother's observation. "I haven't been to church in a while. Usually I work on Sundays."

"Every Sunday?"

"Mom!" Hunter shook her head. "Sorry about that, Tyson."

A smile spread across his lips. "No need to apologize. And to answer your question Mrs. McKay, no, I don't work every Sunday. In fact I'm off this weekend, so you can look for me on Sunday."

"Don't think that I won't," Ingrid said in a serious tone.

Hunter thought it would be best to get her mother out to the car quickly before Ingrid invited Tyson to Sunday dinner or something. "Well, I'll be seeing you, Tyson."

"Same here."

Taking her mother's arm, Hunter led her over to the exit door. She couldn't resist looking over her shoulder. The attractive nurse who had taken care of her mother—the one whose name was Macy Phillips— had approached Tyson and was all in his face. She was touching his arm while chatting away with a huge smile on her face.

Hunter felt a pain stab her heart when she saw that Tyson was smiling back at the woman.

"Well, at least he's not the one who got caught with that girl under the bleachers."

Ingrid's words reclaimed Hunter's attention. She was still holding tight to her mother's arm as they exited the building. "Mom, that was over eighteen years ago. Galen Steele is now married with twins."

"Umm, I guess that means there's hope for those Steele boys yet. I recall they used to have quite a reputation."

Hunter was close to saying that they still did. At

least the single ones. However, she decided to keep her mouth shut.

"So what's going on with you and Dr. Steele?"

Hunter almost missed her step and glanced over at her mother. "What makes you think something is going on?"

Ingrid rolled her eyes. "I wasn't born yesterday, Hunter. I saw the way he was looking at you and the way you were looking at him."

"You're imagining things. Tyson is nothing more than a client."

"If you want me to think so."

Hunter didn't say anything to that. So what if she and Tyson were looking at each other in a way that raised eyebrows? No big deal.

As Hunter opened her car door for her mother, she truly hoped that it wasn't a big deal.

Tyson tossed and turned in the bed, finding it difficult to sleep. Each time he closed his eyes, images of Hunter and that night they spent together flooded his mind. The images were so vivid and powerful that he could lick his lips and taste her there.

Feeling frustration in every part of his body, he slid out of bed and headed for the living room. It seemed that sleep would evade him tonight, so he might as well see what was on television.

Moments later he felt even more frustrated. How could someone have over one hundred channels and not find a single thing of interest on television? He tossed the remote on the table and walked out of the living room into the kitchen, where he opened the refrigerator, needing a beer.

Something had to give, he thought, pulling a beer from the six-pack and popping the tab. Today, answering a page to the ER he had rounded the corner and seen Hunter standing there. Desire the likes of which he'd never felt before had consumed him. And when she'd turned and looked at him, their gazes had met and locked in a way that gave him sensuous shivers just thinking about it.

It didn't make sense. After all he and Hunter had done that night, how in the world could she still be in his system? Or he in hers? He knew the feelings were mutual. He had felt the chemistry, known she had felt it as well. They'd been standing there and he'd been able to actually feel her heat seep into him. It had penetrated every single pore in his body. Neither of them had said a word but their gazes had told it all.

He took a long gulp of his beer but it couldn't wash away the memories. Why was he remembering the way she would whisper his name right before she came, and the way she would scream when caught in the throes of passion? Why was he reliving in his mind all the times his body had straddled hers? Thrust into hers?

And why, considering all of that, was he beginning to believe it wasn't all just about sex? If not sex, then what? Could there be any credence to what Galen had said? That's what Tyson needed to find out before he endured any more sleepless nights.

Leaving the kitchen, he went back into his bedroom and retrieved his cell phone from his nightstand. He glanced over at the clock and saw it was after midnight. Hell, if he couldn't sleep, neither would she. He punched in Hunter's number.

A sleepy voice answered. "Hello?"

"We need to talk, Hunter."

"Tyson?"

He loved hearing her say his name. Even when it was in a lethargic voice it sounded sexy. "What other man would be calling you this time of night?"

"Why are you?"

He couldn't help but smile at her comeback. "I told you. We need to talk."

"Now?"

"No, not now. Tomorrow. I need to drop by your office."

"Fine. Call and make an appointment with Pauline."

"No. I make appointments with you personally. Expect me tomorrow. Good night."

Hunter frowned when she heard the click in her ear. *Expect me tomorrow.* Who did Tyson Steele think he was? Did she even remotely look like that young nurse who'd been all in his face today, flirting and grinning all over the place? Touching his hand? The same one he'd flirted back with? He should be making an appointment with Macy Phillips instead of with her.

And maybe you need to tone down that green streak, Hunter McKay. Jealousy doesn't become you.

She hung up her phone and then slid out of bed to glance over at the clock. Tyson had a lot of nerve calling her at this hour. But then, if there was anything she knew Tyson possessed it was nerve. Right along with an abundance of arrogance.

And what did he want to talk to her about anyway? She preferred continuing on this trend of them not having anything to do with each other. But then that hadn't stopped her from thinking of him. From remembering. From dreaming.

Sliding into her slippers, she went into the kitchen for a cup of tea. Hopefully that would help her sort out a few things in her mind. Her mother's questions hadn't ended at the hospital. Once they'd gotten on the road Ingrid McKay had been determined to uncover all the details she could. The last thing her mother needed to know was that two weekends ago she had turned her bedroom into a real live hot spot. And that Tyson had taught her sexual positions that should be outlawed. Not only that, but all those packs of condoms were also just where he'd left them on the table in her bedroom.

A short while later, as she sat down at her kitchen table sipping her tea, Hunter couldn't stop the shivers that raced through her body at the thought of seeing Tyson again.

Although she had no idea what was on his mind, she had to remember that he only wanted to talk.

Chapter 14

Hunter paced her office, calling herself all kinds of fool for being nervous about Tyson's visit. And she also tried convincing herself the dress she'd chosen to wear to work that morning had nothing to do with knowing he would be dropping by. So what if it was a tad shorter than the ones she normally wore to the office? Tyson telling her how much he liked seeing her legs had nothing to do with it. Nor was that the reason she'd replaced her comfortable pumps with a pair of high heels.

She glanced at her watch. Pauline would be leaving for the day in less than five minutes. Had Tyson deliberately timed his arrival when he figured they would be alone? She shook her head, telling herself she was jumping to conclusions. Tyson's visit to her office might just be strictly business. There was a possibility he had questions about those preliminary house plans. Yes, those same house plans she'd already dismissed as inconsequential. She knew he had no more intention of building a house in the country than she did. But she had put her time, concentration and energy into them. That was why she had billed him for them anyway. And she hadn't been cheap. He could be questioning the size of his bill, but a personal visit wasn't needed for that.

The buzzer on her desk sounded and she inhaled deeply before crossing the room to push the button. "Yes, Pauline?"

"I'm about to leave, Hunter. Do you need me to do anything before I—"

When she heard a voice in the background she knew her conversation with Pauline was being interrupted by someone. "Excuse me, Hunter. But Dr. Steele is here. He said you are expecting him."

There was no need to tell Pauline to send him in because at that moment, her office door opened and Tyson walked in. She glared at him, a little put out that he assumed he could just walk into her office whenever he felt like it. But then that thought faded from her mind when her eyes roamed over him. No man could wear a pair of jeans better.

Nor could a man remove them better, either.

She tried not to remember that night in her apartment when he had stripped out of his jeans for her. Remembering also made her recall just what he was packing behind the zipper of those jeans.

"If there's nothing else you need for me to do then I'll see you tomorrow, Hunter."

At that moment she realized she still had Pauline on the line. "That's fine, Pauline. Enjoy your evening and I'll see you tomorrow."

She clicked off the line and lifted her chin at Tyson, but before she could give him a piece of her mind, he asked, "How's your mother?"

"Mom's fine. Thanks for asking." So, okay, it was nice of him to inquire…but still. "It would have been nice if you'd given me a time as to when to expect you, Tyson."

He actually looked remorseful. "Sorry about that. It was late last night when I called you and—"

"Trust me. I know how late it was."

A small smile touched his lips as he leaned back against the closed door. "I couldn't sleep and figured if I couldn't sleep you shouldn't be able to sleep, either. Sounds pretty juvenile, doesn't it?"

"Yes, especially since I wasn't responsible for your inability to sleep."

He straightened and took a few steps into the middle of the room. Hunter's stomach immediately knotted and her breathing suddenly seemed forced. The man was testosterone personified. And why did those thighs, those hard muscular thighs that had ridden her so many times, look perfect in his jeans?

"But you are responsible, Hunter," he said, interrupting her intense appraisal of him. "That's why I'm here."

Hunter frowned. What he was saying didn't make much sense. "Okay, so you can't sleep at night and for some reason you think I'm to blame. If that's the case, what do you expect me to do about it?"

"Give me a week. I want a week in your bed since a mere night didn't do a damn thing to eradicate you from my system."

Tyson looked at the beautiful woman with the shocked look on her face. At some point he needed to stop astonishing her this way. He'd gotten the same re-action from her that night at Notorious after stating his plans to seduce her.

He shoved his hands into his pockets, readying him-self for what was to come. She could get mad or glad. Either way he intended to get his week. Hell, he needed that week. When time ticked by and she didn't say any-thing, just sat behind her desk and gazed at him like he was stone crazy, he finally asked, "Well?"

Tyson knew he'd pushed too hard when a furious ex-pression finally overtook her expression. She eased out of her chair to come around her desk and stand in front of him with her hands planted firmly on her hips. He could actually see fire in those gorgeous brown eyes of hers and should have had enough sense to step back, but he didn't. The way he saw it, he didn't have anything to lose at this point and he intended to stand his ground.

"You sex-crazed womanizing ass!" she said in a loud, angry voice. "What's wrong, Dr. Steele? That little nurse didn't work out for you so you thought you could just show up here demanding more sex from me because you need it? Let me tell you just where you can—"

"I don't just need sex, Hunter," he interrupted her in a voice that matched her volume. "I need *you*. And what little nurse are you talking about?"

"I'm talking about that ER nurse who was flirting with you yesterday. And I saw you flirting back."

A fierce frown covered Tyson's face when she brought up Macy Phillips. "For your information, Macy Phillips was on my 'to do' list, along with several other women," he snapped.

"Then by all means do them. What's stopping you?" she snapped back, getting in his face.

"You're stopping me, dammit, and I don't know why," he retorted, hating he had to admit such a thing. "Ever since that night I saw you at Notorious, I haven't wanted another woman. I haven't thought of anyone else. I figured that once I made love to you my life would return to normal. But things have gotten worse for me. For some reason you aren't out my system. I dream about you at night. I think about you during the day. My cleaning lady has been to my place twice since that night you were there for dinner, but I swear I can still smell your scent."

To Tyson's surprise Hunter took a step back. It was as if his words had finally gotten to her, were now sinking in. So he decided to plunge forward. "So I came up with a plan."

"Another one?" she asked flippantly.

"Yes, another one," he said, more than a little agitated. "There has to be a reason I can't get enough of you, and whether you want to admit it or not, I'm not out of your system, either. I can tell. Anyone who's within ten feet of us can pick up on the strong sexual chemistry between us. I think your mother even picked up on something."

"She did," Hunter said in a somewhat calmer tone. "I told her there was nothing going on between us but I don't think she believes me."

Then, as if she realized she'd gone soft, her spine straightened and her voice became firm. "And don't you dare stand there and tell me what I don't have out of my system. You have no way of knowing that."

He lifted his chin. "Don't I?"

She crossed her arms over her chest. "No, you don't."

"Are you saying that you don't still want me? That you don't go to bed with thoughts of me inside of you? Kissing you? Tasting you? Riding you hard?"

He saw heat flare in her eyes at his words. He also saw blatant desire that fanned the flames of what he was feeling. "Well, are you?"

She squared her shoulders and glared at him. "I'm not saying anything."

"Then it's admission by omission."

"I am *not* admitting to anything. If I'm not out of your system then that's your problem, one you need to deal with on your own. Contrary to what you seem to think, you're out of my system, Tyson. Nothing you say or do will prove otherwise," she said haughtily.

A slow smile spread across his features. "You think not?"

Hunter didn't like his tone, nor the "let me prove differently" look in Tyson's eyes. For once she felt she might have said too much, tossed out a dare she hadn't intended to make. And now he had that predatory look on his face. The one that meant he intended to prove her wrong. She took a few more steps back and came to a stop when her backside hit against her desk.

"Isn't tonight Thursday? You're having dinner with your folks, right?" she asked.

"What about it?"

During their talk over wine and cheese in her bedroom, he mentioned that over the years his mother had insisted on Thursday dinners as a way to show her six sons that married life would be wonderful. Tyson had stated that as far as he was concerned, the only thing his mother was showing him was what a great cook she continued to be. For him it was the delicious meals that were the draw.

"I wouldn't want you to be late for dinner," she told him.

A smiled curved his lips. "Are you trying to get rid of me, Hunter?"

She leaned back against her desk. "What do you think?"

"I think it's time I show you that you want me as much as I want you."

A slow stirring erupted in the pit of her stomach when Tyson began walking toward her. His expression was serious, his eyes dark and honed in on hers. Her heart pounded in her chest with every step he took. She was tempted to run, but her feet felt cemented in place. Besides, from the look on Tyson's face she knew that he wouldn't think twice about chasing after her.

Did she even want to run?

She frowned at the doubt that clouded her mind. Of course she wanted to run, to escape, to get the hell out of here. *Umm, maybe not*, she thought when Tyson stopped and kicked off his shoes and then took the time to remove his socks.

Hunter had a pretty good idea where this was going, and a part of her wanted it more than anything. She hadn't been completely honest by claiming he was out of her system. But a week-long affair wasn't necessarily the answer. It might work for him, but she ran the risk that he'd get even more under her skin.

As she continued to look at Tyson, he straightened and went for his shirt, undoing the buttons and easing it from his chest and broad muscular shoulders. Hunter tried not to remember the feel of that chest rubbing against her hardened nipples, but she failed. She heard herself moan.

"You said something, Hunter?" he asked, staring at her with a predatory look.

She swallowed and shook her head, unable to speak for a moment. When she could, she said, "No, I didn't say anything." But she knew she should. She should speak up and put an end to this madness. But a part of her was curious to see just how far he would go before she sent him packing.

And speaking of packing... He eased his jeans down his legs to reveal a pair of sexy briefs and it was obvious just what he was packing between those massive thighs.

"Is there a reason you're removing your clothes in my office?" she asked, deciding she needed to say something before he went any further.

He smiled over at her as he inserted his fingers in the waistband of his briefs. "Yes, there's a reason."

And then, without saying another word, he lowered his briefs and showed her the reason. In all its arousing and throbbing glory.

As far as Tyson was concerned, the worst thing Hunter could do at that moment was lick her lips. Major bad timing on her part. Especially when he saw the sexual hunger in her eyes.

Then she lifted her chin. "I won't be removing my clothes, Tyson."

He stood in front of her totally naked and he couldn't help noticing she had a hard time zeroing in on his face. Instead her gaze kept straying to his groin. "I don't recall asking you to take your clothes off, Hunter, mainly because I intend to take them off for you."

She narrowed her eyes at him. "You wouldn't dare."

He chuckled. "I would. And I will." He took a step toward her.

"If you come any closer, I'll scream," she threatened.

His mouth curved into a smile. "Baby, you're going to be screaming anyway, so one more scream is a moot point." He trailed a finger down her thigh. "You want to convince me you didn't wear this short dress just for me?"

"Think whatever you want."

"In that case, I think you did wear it just for me," he said, loving the feel of his fingers on her bare skin. "And I want to thank you properly for doing so." Then Tyson lowered his mouth to hers.

Hunter knew the moment Tyson's tongue touched hers there would be nothing proper about this kiss. She was proven right when he began devouring her mouth with an intensity that had her fighting back moans. Pushing him away was not even a consideration. Instead, she eased up on tiptoe and wrapped her arms around his neck to deepen the kiss.

When his hand began easing up her dress, instinctively, her legs spread apart. Just like the last time, his touch was like an aphrodisiac, making her crave things she shouldn't have but wanted anyway. And topping the list was Tyson. She wanted him doing all those naughty and sinful yet delicious things to her.

Her thoughts were suddenly snatched from her mind when Tyson's fingers settled between her legs. Oh, yes, she remembered these fingers and just what they could do to her, how they could make her feel. He knew how to work them with a skill she found astounding. The man had an uncanny ability to take her breath away.

He broke off the kiss and stared down at her, deliberately holding her gaze while his fingers worked their magic inside her, making her moan, gasp and then moan again. "You sure you want this?" he asked in a deep, husky voice. "After all, you claim I'm the only one with the problem. That I am out of your system."

Hunter knew he was toying with her, trying to make her admit something she had adamantly refuted. "You're wet, Hunter," he said, moving his fingers in slow, circular motions inside her. "I like stirring you up this way, and do you know why?"

She fought the urge to ask but failed. "No, why?"

"Because doing so escalates your scent. There is something about your scent that's powerful and intoxicating. It arouses me whenever I'm around you. Makes me want to taste you here," he said, inserting an additional finger inside her. "I miss tasting you that way."

She didn't want to admit it but that particular part of her body missed being tasted that way, too. His fingers and tongue should be considered weapons of mass seduction. He held tight to her gaze, daring her to look away, while his fingers slowly and provocatively began pushing her over the edge. "Am I out of your system, Hunter?"

Did he really need for her to answer that? Especially when her nipples had hardened and her hips moved with the rhythm of his fingers. She drew in a deep breath and shook her head.

"Not good enough. I want to hear you say it," Tyson said as he leaned down close to her lips just seconds before his tongue swiped across them. "Say it, Hunter."

There was no way she could refuse him. Not now when he'd whipped her body into a need she could not deny. "No, you're not out of my system."

Her words made an arrogant smile touch his lips. "Glad we're in agreement about that." He pulled his fingers from inside her and instantly she felt bereft. And then he was pulling her dress over her head, skillfully removing her bra in the process. His hands were there to cup her breasts the moment they were free. "Beautiful," he whispered huskily. "I missed these girls. They spoiled me."

No, in all honesty, he had spoiled them, Hunter thought. And they had definitely missed him. When he sucked a nipple into his mouth, she knew he was about to spoil them some more. She drew in a deep breath and struggled to hold herself up when she was about to slither to the floor. Tyson came to her rescue then, grabbing her by the hips to hoist her onto her desk.

"Now to get to what we both want," he said, using the tips of his fingers to trace a path toward her inner thighs. Hunter felt her heart pick up a beat when his hand closed possessively over her feminine mound through her lace panties.

"You like lace, I notice," he said throatily.

"Yes, I like lace," she responded, barely able to get the words out.

"That's good to know."

Hunter was about to ask why he thought so when he tugged on her panties and automatically she lifted her hips so he could ease them down her legs. Once that was done he captured her gaze as he gripped her hips and moved forward, leading the head of his engorged erection toward her womanly entrance.

He was almost there when common sense invaded her mind. "Stop!"

He loosened his hold on her. "Stop?" he repeated with an incredulous look on his face.

She nodded. "Condom."

The shocked look in his eyes let her know he couldn't believe he'd been less than an inch from entering her without having given any thought to protection. "Condom. Right," he said, slowly backing away to retrieve a packet from the jeans he'd tossed on the floor. "Thanks for the reminder. This has never happened to me before."

Hunter believed him and unashamedly watched as he expertly sheathed his erection. Looking back over at her, he said, "Ready to pick up where we left off?"

"Yes." She was more than ready. Shivers raced through her body at the intense desire she saw in the depths of his green eyes as he headed back toward her. And to show him just how ready she was, she boldly spread her legs. She'd never been taken on a desk before and was curious to see how they would pull it off.

When he returned, he said, "Grab my shoulders and hold on tight."

He lifted her hips, guiding his erection unerringly inside her. She threw her head back and moaned at the impact. Her inner muscles clenched, tightening around him. Tyson being back inside her felt good. Like he belonged there.

She swallowed, wondering how she could allow her mind to think that when it came to Tyson. A man whose favorite pastime was bedding women. All thoughts fled her mind when he began thrusting into her in long, hard strokes. The intensity of them shook her to the core. She understood why he told her to grab his shoulders when he began pounding into her at the same time he eased her back on the desk, nearly covering her body with his. Luckily, she had a big desk because they needed the space.

Suddenly Hunter's body jerked from what seemed like an electrical shock that traveled through her body straight to her nerve endings. It was all she needed to push her over the edge. And Tyson joined her. She released a guttural scream mere seconds before he leaned in and took her mouth with a greedy kiss that swallowed up her cry. Just when she came down to earth, he moved against her again and she was hurled into yet another orgasm. Why had she ever claimed to be over this man?

"Glad we're in agreement about that week."

Hunter glanced over at Tyson as she slid back into her dress. He had gotten dressed and was leaning against her desk watching her do the same. No, they weren't in agreement since she hadn't agreed to anything. "We had tonight, Tyson. That's the best I can do."

"I want a week."

"You got tonight."

"I want a week, Hunter."

He was persistent. After smoothing her dress down her body she stared at him. "Why, Tyson? What will a week do for you?"

"I'm convinced I'm a man possessed."

Hunter raised a brow. "Possessed?"

"Yes, possessed by passion. Yours."

Now she'd heard everything. She barely knew all the things to do in the bedroom so how could an experienced man like him get obsessed with her? It didn't make much sense. She opened her mouth to ask the question but his words stopped her.

"Please don't ask me to explain it, Hunter, because I can't. All I know is that you're the only woman I want and I need to know what we just did won't be the last time. I need that week. I'll even let you call the shots and set the grounds rules during that week if that's what it takes. But I've got to get you out of my system for good."

She hated to ask but she had to. "But what if that one week doesn't work?"

He stared at her without saying anything, and she realized that in his mind it was simply not an option. "We'll think positive. It has to work."

She didn't say anything for a minute as she remembered what they'd just done on her desk. A week of Tyson wouldn't kill her. Besides, if she was honest with herself, she would admit that a part of her wanted him just as badly. She had craved his touch, had dreamed of him inside her. However, she wouldn't go so far as to say she was possessed. She just hoped the week gave him what he wanted. Freedom from her once and for all.

"Fine. You'll get your week, Tyson, but I'm setting the ground rules. If you think you're going to keep me on my back 24/7 then you're wrong. We will do other things."

He arched his brow. "Other things like what?"

"I'll think of something."

"Yes, you do that, Hunter. In the meantime…"

He crossed the room to her, leaned forward and captured her lips with his.

Chapter 15

There had to be a reason he couldn't get enough of Hunter, Tyson thought, recalling how after making love to her on her desk, they had gotten dressed only to end up making love a second time on the sofa in her office.

And how could he have almost forgotten to use a condom that first time? That was something he'd never done before with any woman. He had truly acted like a man possessed and he needed to get his life back on track. If he didn't know better he would think Hunter was a witch. A beautiful, delicious and sensuous witch who was wreaking havoc on his brain cells to the point where he couldn't think straight. Hell, he wasn't thinking at all. When had he ever wanted to go a full week with any woman? But with him it hadn't been an option. It had been about survival. And that's what bothered him more than anything. When had he ever admitted to a woman that she was in his system like he was some kind of sex addict or something? Why hadn't he been able to let go and walk away like he'd done with all the others? For the umpteenth time he had to ask himself, what made Hunter so different?

"You're quiet tonight, Tyson."

He glanced down the dinner table. Of course it had to be Mercury who noticed. "Don't have anything to say."

He had arrived late at his parents' house for dinner. He knew his mother assumed he'd gotten detained at the hospital, but that was far from the truth. He had arrived in time to see the photos Galen and Brittany had been passing around of the twins, which had, luckily, deflected any questions about why he'd been late.

He noted these Thursday dinners were getting rather large with three of his brothers now married. And for the first time the grandkids were present, which had to be the reason his mother was smiling all over the place. Not to mention the growing family had given her an excuse to buy a new dining room table, one that seated fourteen people. Tyson could do the math. It was quite apparent that Eden Tyson Steele was counting on her three bachelor sons producing wives to fill the vacant seats at the table one day.

"Oh, you're in one of those moods," Gannon said, grinning. "That's what happens when you prepare dinner for a woman."

That got everyone's attention. "You prepared dinner?" Galen asked, surprised. Anyone who knew him knew he didn't cook for himself, much less for anyone else.

"I ordered take-out. No big deal."

"You actually fed a woman?" Jonas asked, staring at him with disbelief.

He glared at his brother. "Like I said, Jonas, no big deal." Usually he didn't get agitated easily, especially with his siblings, but for some reason tonight he was. He should be overjoyed Hunter had granted him another week, but there was that risk that it wouldn't be enough. Then where would he be?

"I ran into Ingrid McKay today at the grocery store," his mother said, eyeing him speculatively. "You didn't mention that Hunter McKay had moved back to town."

He stared at his mother, wondering why she would bring that up...especially now. And as far as mentioning it to her, he hadn't known she even knew Hunter. Had she kept a log of every girl he'd hit on in high school? "I didn't mention it because I didn't think it was a big deal. I didn't even know you knew Hunter."

"Of course I know Hunter. She was Reverend McKay's granddaughter. She sang in the choir and had an awesome voice. I also recall she was a beautiful girl with impeccable manners. How could I not know her when we attended the same church?"

But so did four hundred other people, Tyson thought, taking a sip of his iced tea.

According to his mother Hunter had a nice voice. He'd heard Hunter scream a lot of times but never sing. Nor could he recall her singing whenever he attended church back in the day. Must have been those Sundays when he'd dozed off during the service.

"Hunter McKay," Jonas said, smiling. "I remember

her from high school. We graduated together. Isn't she the one who dumped you, Tyson?"

Tyson glared at Jonas for the second time that night. "She didn't dump me."

"That's not the way I heard it," Galen said, grinning.

"Well, you heard wrong."

Brittany, who seemed to have acquired the role of peacemaker since marrying Galen, spoke up and changed the subject. "I forgot to mention that Jonas wants to use the twins in his next marketing campaign. Isn't that wonderful?"

Tyson gave Brittany an appreciative smile. Everyone at the table got so caught up with her announcement that any further conversation about Tyson and Hunter was abruptly forgotten.

He took a sip of his tea and glanced across the table at Eli, who was looking at him with a grin on his face. Eli was the only one who'd known of his plan to pursue Hunter. He was grateful Eli was the brother who knew how to keep his mouth shut, although he liked giving his opinion much too often to suit Tyson. He couldn't help wondering what Eli found amusing since he still had that silly-looking grin on his face. Then Tyson remembered. Eli had warned him about getting possessed by passion. Damn. For once he wished he'd taken his brother's warning to heart. Now he had a feeling he was way over his head where Hunter was concerned.

Hunter began drying off her body with the huge towel. She much preferred taking showers, but tonight a good hot soak had done wonders for her body, a body that had gone through intense lovemaking with Tyson Steele.

She hadn't counted on him taking her on her desk and her sofa, all in the same afternoon. In all honesty, she hadn't counted on being taken at all.

And now she had agreed to spend a week with him. Because of that decision she could see herself taking even more baths. But like she'd told him, their week would be filled with more than just lovemaking. One sure way to get her out of his system, if she was as deeply embedded into it as he claimed, was to come up with activities he didn't do with women. The thought made her smile. In the end he would thank her.

His admission still baffled her. Personally, if she felt possessed by any man he would certainly be the last one to know it. But Tyson had pretty much placed his cards on the table without any care as to how she played them. Just as long as he got his week with her. That was the craziest thing she'd ever heard.

Still, she couldn't discount the changes making love with Tyson had done to her and for her. Thanks to him she now knew firsthand just what an ass Carter had been, especially in the bedroom. And thanks to Tyson she had discovered a lot about her own sexuality. He'd opened a door to sensual exploration and adventure for her. With Tyson nothing was taboo, nothing was off-limits or forbidden. He wouldn't be the only one using this week to his advantage. She would, too, but for different reasons. For her it would be a week of sexual journeys and sensuous excursions. But the big question for her was how to keep her emotions out of the equation.

For Tyson this was about sex and nothing more and she had to remember that. More than once she'd felt a pull at her heart whenever they made love. She had to fight hard not to get lust mixed up with love.

Hunter had slid into her nightgown and was about to grab a magazine off her coffee table to read in bed when the sound of her doorbell startled her. She could think of only one person showing up at her place tonight. Hadn't they made love twice already today? He'd warned her that he was a greedy ass. Now she was beginning to believe him.

Dismissing the rush of desire moving up her spine, she put down the magazine and went to her door. A quick look out the peephole confirmed her suspicions. It was Tyson.

She fought back the sensations she felt just knowing he was on the other side of that door. The thought that she was beginning to be just as insatiable as he didn't sit well with her. Releasing a deep sigh mixed with frustration and desire, she opened the door.

He stood there and held her gaze. Although she didn't want to, her body felt heated from his deep, penetrating stare. Blood was rushing to every part of her body and she knew there was no way to stop it. Instead of saying anything, she moved aside for him to enter. And when he walked past her she inhaled his rich, masculine scent. The same one she'd washed off her skin less than an hour ago.

He paused in the middle of her living room. Hunter was surprised he hadn't just headed straight for the bedroom. Tyson was arrogant enough to do so. He turned and she felt the heat of his gaze as it moved up and down her baby-doll nightgown.

"Believe it or not, Hunter, this isn't a booty call," he finally said, breaking the silence.

She leaned back against her closed door. "Is there a new name for it now?" She wouldn't be surprised if he'd coined his own term.

"I didn't come here to make love to you…although I have no qualms about doing so if you want."

She crossed her arms over her chest and ignored how his gaze moved to her breasts. She felt her nipples harden. "Then why are you here?"

A smile touched the corners of his lips, so adorable she had to blink to make sure it was real. "I decided to drop by tonight, Hunter, because I want to hear you sing."

Tyson loved Hunter's facial expressions whenever he caught her off guard. He'd shocked her again. Without waiting for an invitation he took a seat on her sofa.

"Sing?" she asked. "What makes you think I can sing?"

"My mother. She mentioned it over dinner." At another shocked look, he smiled. They just kept on coming.

"Why would your mother bring up my name at dinner?" she asked, leaving her place at the door to sit down in the wingback chair in the living room.

"She ran into your mother at the grocery store and found out you'd moved back to town. She wanted to know why I hadn't mentioned it to her. I told her I didn't even know she knew you. That's when she said you used to be in the choir at church and had a nice voice."

Hunter smiled. "That was kind of her to think so. I'm surprised she remembered. That was years ago."

Tyson chuckled. "My mother rarely forgets anything, trust me. So are you going to sing for me?"

"No."

"Why not?"

"Other than humming occasionally when I take a shower, I haven't sung in years."

"So? I'd like to hear you sing."

"Why?"

Tyson wasn't sure. All he knew was that when he left his parents' home he had wanted to come straight here and get her to sing for him. "I just want to hear you, that's all."

She stared at him for a minute and he knew she was trying to figure him out. He wanted to tell her not to waste her time, when lately even he hadn't been able to figure out his actions, at least not when it came to her.

"Fine," she finally said. "Is there a particular song you want to hear?"

"Anything by Whitney Houston."

He saw the smile that spread across her lips and it stirred his insides. "Throw me a real challenge, will you? But okay, I got this. Lucky for you I happen to love all her songs." Easing from her chair, she grinned. "I really feel silly doing this, but you asked for it. Here goes."

And then while he watched she threw her head back, closed her eyes and began belting out "The Greatest Love of All."

Tyson sat there spellbound, mesmerized and totally captivated. His mother was right. Hunter had an awesome voice and listening to her sing touched him deeply. There were so many facets of Hunter McKay and he wondered if her husband had appreciated every single one. Apparently not.

He couldn't take his eyes off her, standing there in the middle of her living room, singing for him and him alone. She appeared shrouded in sensuality and his pulse throbbed at the effect she was having on him. It was crazy. It didn't make much sense. Yet it was happening. Hunter McKay was drawing everything out of him and without very much effort.

Moments later when she finished and opened her eyes, she stared across the room at him, a tentative smile touching her lips. "Okay. I'm done."

Tyson knew in all honesty, so was he. Hunter had done him in. He felt his heart pounding in his chest. She looked beautiful standing there in her short lacy nightgown that showed off a pair of beautiful legs. It sounded crazy but he was beginning to think this entire thing with Hunter was more than her being deeply embedded in his system. It was more than him being possessed by her passion. And he needed this week to figure it out.

Standing, he clapped his hands. "Bravo. You were excellent. Superb. If you ever quit your day job you can—"

"Become a backup singer for Prince? That was my childhood dream for the longest time."

He chuckled. "Was it?"

"Yes."

"If you didn't make it, then it was his loss." He crossed the room to her. "Thanks for singing for me. Mom was right. I had no idea. You have a beautiful voice."

She shrugged. "Carter never thought so. He claimed I always sang off-key."

Tyson shook his head. "The more I hear about your ex-husband, the more I believe you were right."

She raised a brow. "About what?"

"About him being a bastard." He then leaned down and placed a light kiss on her lips. "Walk me to the door."

Another shocked look appeared on her face. "You're leaving?"

"Yes." He took her hand as he headed toward the door. "I have surgeries in the morning, but call me tomorrow afternoon to let me know of your plans for our weekend. I have the entire weekend off."

"All right."

Before he opened the door he couldn't resist taking her into his arms and devouring her mouth. He knew leaving her alone tonight would be hard but it was something he had to do. Hunter was a puzzle he had to piece together for his peace of mind.

When he released her mouth, he whispered against her moist lips. "Good night."

"Good night, Tyson."

And then he opened the door and walked out.

Chapter 16

"This is Dr. Steele. May I help you?"

Hunter loved the sexy sound of Tyson's voice. "Yes, Dr. Steele, this is Hunter and you can definitely help me."

She heard the richness of his chuckle and wished it didn't make her pulse rate increase. "And what can I do for you, Ms. McKay?"

"I thought we'd take in a movie tonight. Anything you prefer seeing?"

There was silence on his end and Hunter knew why. Rumor had it that if Tyson Steele took a woman out, his bedroom was as far as they got. This week wouldn't be status quo for him. He'd said she could set the ground rules and she had.

"Doesn't matter," he finally said. "Anything you

want to see will be fine with me. I'll pick you up at seven. Is that a good time for dinner and a movie?"

She was surprised at his suggestion of dinner. "Yes, seven is fine. I'll see you then."

"And, Hunter?"

"Yes?"

"Bring your dancing shoes. I want to take you dancing after the movie."

He wanted to take her dancing? "Okay." After ending her call with Tyson, Hunter leaned back in her office chair as she remembered his visit to her apartment last night. No booty call, he'd just wanted to hear her sing. How strange was that? Had he asked to spend the night she probably would have let him. But he hadn't asked.

She hated admitting it, but Tyson Steele was beginning to confuse her. Like his suggestion of dinner, dancing and him picking her up. She'd honestly assumed that he would ask what time the movie started and say he would meet her there. Anything else would constitute a real date, and Tyson Steele didn't do real dates. He'd told her that himself during their little bedroom talk that night over wine and cheese. He claimed dating would encourage women to get the wrong ideas regarding the nature of his intent.

So why this sudden change of behavior? She could only assume that he figured she knew the score so she wasn't anyone he had to worry about. He was trying to work her out of his system and nothing more.

She looked at her watch. If Tyson was going to take her to dinner, a movie and dancing, she needed to make a few shopping stops before going home. Her goal was to make this a week neither of them would forget. And tonight was the kickoff.

"You dance as well as you sing," Tyson whispered to Hunter hours later when he led her to the center of the floor for another dance. This one was a slow number. About time, he thought, as he pulled her into his arms. He was beginning to think line dancing was all they'd be doing tonight.

"Thanks. I love to dance."

Tyson could tell. Even when they'd sat out a few she had moved from side to side in her chair, keeping time with the music.

He had picked her up promptly at seven and when she opened the door he had to stand there for a moment to get his bearings. From head to toe, she looked fabulous. And he had told her so many more times than he probably should have tonight. He totally liked her short, tight-fitting dress and killer heels.

They had dined at Toni's, an Italian restaurant located in the heart of the city. Over dinner she had told him about the additional clients she had acquired and again thanked him for the three he had referred. He was glad everything seemed to be working out for her.

Tyson wrapped his arms around her, loving the feel of holding her as they moved slowly around the dance floor. Tonight had been great and he had enjoyed her company. He'd even enjoyed the movie she'd chosen for them to see. He was surprised to discover that, like him, she liked Westerns. This one had been one of the good ones and had held his attention most of the time.

Hunter held it all the other times. He had to admit he'd enjoyed sitting beside her in the theater, sharing popcorn with her. Holding her hand.

She pressed her cheek against his chest as they slowly swayed to the music. Their movements were so slow that at times it appeared neither of them was moving. And their bodies were so close he could feel her every curve. He was getting sexually charged just thinking about tonight and how it would end. Again, she'd made it clear that she would not spend a single night this week in his bed, and he had no problem wearing out the mattress at her place if that's what she preferred.

Resting his cheek against the top of her head, he couldn't help but think there was more to his relationship with Hunter than just great sex. Dinner and the movie had proven that and he looked forward to spending more time with her outside the bedroom this week.

When he felt her stiffen in his arms, he glanced down at her. "You all right?"

She glanced up and met his gaze. "My ex is here."

Tyson lifted a brow. "Your ex? Here?"

"Yes. I heard he might be coming to Phoenix on business, and I can only assume that's why he's here. He just walked in with a group of men."

Tyson nodded. "If his presence makes you uncomfortable, we can leave."

She shook her head. "No. He's seen us and maybe that's good thing."

"Why?"

"My mother-in-law overheard Carter's plan to contact me while he's here and play on my heartstrings."

"Your heartstrings?"

"Yes. He has this crazy notion that since I hadn't dated since our divorce that I'm still in love with him and would take him back, even after all he's done."

Tyson didn't know what all the man had done, but just from the time he had spent with Hunter he knew she felt only loathing for her ex. "You say he's seen us?"

"Yes. In fact he's sitting at the table, staring at us now."

"Good."

Tyson pulled Hunter closer into his arms, leaned down and covered her mouth with his.

Hunter suddenly sat straight up in bed. When she saw a naked Tyson sleeping beside her, she realized it hadn't been a dream at all. They'd gone to dinner, a movie and dancing. The evening had gone great. Not even seeing Carter had put a damper on things, because Tyson had refused to let it.

Although it had been pretense, he had gone out of his way to give the impression that the two of them were a hot item. In addition to kissing her in the middle of the dance floor, when they had returned to their table Tyson had taken her in his lap and hand-fed her the chips and dip they'd ordered. She couldn't help but enjoy Tyson's attentiveness, even if it was playacting. He had lavished her with attention and affection. Tonight Tyson had made her feel significant, appreciated and desired right before Carter's eyes.

From the angry look she'd seen on her ex's face, he'd gotten the message Tyson had intended. The message

that she belonged to Tyson. And in a way she did…
even if it was for just a week. They had left the nightclub only after Carter had done so, satisfied their mis-
sion had been accomplished.

The moment they had entered her apartment Tyson
had swept her off her feet and carried her into the bedroom. There he had undressed her and his skilled body
had taken her over the edge. Not once. Or twice. Three
times before they'd finally drifted off to sleep.

Smiling now, she settled back down in bed and snuggled her body deeper into his. Why was she allowing
herself to get wrapped up in the moment?

And why tonight, when she had seen Carter again
after all this time, had she felt nothing…absolutely nothing? It seemed her mind, body and soul refused to waste
any more emotions—loathing or otherwise—on the
man she'd spent eight years trying and failing to satisfy. But now, thanks to Tyson, she knew the failures
weren't her fault, but were Carter's.

She drew in a deep breath. In Tyson's mind, he had
wanted another week with her because he believed he
was possessed by passion. And she would admit the
two of them could generate a lot of that. But now she
could finally admit to herself the reason she'd agreed
to a week with him. She had fallen in love with him.

It really didn't matter how it happened or when but
she knew it had. She wanted to believe it happened the
first time they'd made love. He had treated her like a
woman who deserved to be treated with dignity and re-
spect. But he'd gone even further by treating her like a
woman who deserved to be appreciated. Each and every

time they made love he'd made her feel special, like a woman worth having, even in the bedroom.

It didn't bother her that he didn't return her love or that he would never know her true feelings for him. Loving him was her secret. After this week was over and he returned to his world—the one filled with all those other women—she would always have these precious memories.

"You okay?"

She glanced over at Tyson. She hadn't meant to awaken him. "Yes, I'm fine."

"Baby, I know you're fine. That dress you wore tonight showed just how fine you are."

She chuckled. "You liked my dress?"

"I told you I did. A number of times. I like every outfit you put on your body. And I like your body, as well."

"Do you?"

"Yes, I do."

She eased out of his arms to straddle him. "Your erection is rock-hard. I definitely want to put something like that to good use."

"And your girls wants my attention," he said, reaching upward to cup the twin mounds in his hands. "I plan to put them to good use, as well."

"Not before I give you a little attention, Mr. Steele."

And then she eased down in bed and took his shaft into her mouth. He grabbed hold of her shoulders to pull her back up, but she figured the feel of her lips and tongue pleasuring him enticed him to change his mind. Instead he let his fingers tunnel through the curls on her head as he began groaning deep in his throat.

"Hunter! You got to stop. I'm about to come."

She recalled giving him a similar warning one night that he'd ignored just like she intended to do. Instead of stopping, she took him deeper and suckled him right into an orgasm.

"Hunter!"

A short while later she lifted her head and looked up at him and smiled. In her heart she knew she loved him but he would never know.

"You, Hunter McKay, are a naughty girl," he said throatily.

"And you, Tyson Steele," she said, licking her lips, "are one delicious man."

"Tell me about your ex-husband," Tyson said, holding Hunter in his arms. It had taken him a minute to recover from the orgasm she'd given him. It had been explosive and left his entire body reeling.

Hunter lifted her head and he could see the surprise in her eyes. If she found his request odd, then she wasn't alone. He'd never asked a woman about her ex. Usually her past didn't matter. It certainly didn't have any bearing on the present. But with Hunter it mattered. He'd seen Carter Robinson tonight and other than what Eli had told him, Tyson didn't know everything the man had done.

She didn't say anything for a long moment, and then she finally spoke. "I guess after tonight I owe you an explanation."

"No explanation needed. You told me why you needed him to see us together. The heartstrings thing.

But I want to know about him. I'm having a hard time understanding what man in his right mind would let such a passionate woman like you get away."

She snuggled deeper in his arms, as if she needed his closeness to tell him what he wanted to know. "That's just it. Carter never thought of me as passionate." She paused a moment. "We met at a party a couple of years after I finished grad school. We dated for a year and he asked me to marry him. I thought we were perfect together. We shared the same profession and the same dreams and goals. Three years after we were married I discovered he was having an affair with a former client. He asked for my forgiveness, said it wouldn't happen again. But it did. By then he didn't care that I knew and said if I left him I would have more to lose than he did. I believed him, so I stayed, although we didn't share a bed. I moved into the guest room."

She drew in a deep breath. "Things continued that way for two years until I hired a private investigator who uncovered a number of things, including the fact that while I slept in the guest room upstairs, Carter would on occasion sneak his mistress into the house to spend the night with her in our bed."

Anger flared through Tyson at the thought of any man disrespecting his wife that way. No wonder she had a problem with sharing a bed with him where she'd known other women had been before her. "Did you confront him about it?"

"Yes, and I told him I was divorcing him. He laughed, and said I didn't have the backbone to do such a thing. He saw how wrong he was the day he was served the divorce papers. Everyone turned against me for divorcing him. His family. People I thought were our friends. And then on top of all that, he set out to hurt me by taking my clients and making things difficult for me in Boston." She drew in a deep breath. "In a way my brother's request that I come home to help with our parents gave me the perfect excuse to return to Phoenix to start over."

While he listened, Hunter also told him how during her marriage her ex had tried eroding what little self-confidence she had. How he had tried making it seem that his involvement with other women was her fault and how he'd tried controlling her. "And to think Carter actually believed I could still love him and he could get me back after all he did." He could hear the sadness in her voice as she spoke.

Tyson didn't say anything as he continued to hold her in his arms. He felt a huge sense of protectiveness swell inside him where Hunter was concerned, and knew at that moment he would never give any man the chance to hurt her ever again.

Chapter 17

"What's this I hear about you making a fool of yourself with a woman, Tyson? You've been seen around town on several occasions, taking her to dinner, movies, dancing and concerts. I even heard you attended church with her one Sunday."

Tyson had known when he'd opened the door to find Mercury standing there that there had to be a reason for his visit. "And what of it?"

"Acting all infatuated with a woman is not like you."

Yes, Tyson agreed. Mercury was right, it wasn't like him. But he had discovered his interest in Hunter had gone beyond just the physical. It was a lot more than being possessed by the passion they could generate, as he'd assumed. What was supposed to last only one week was now going into its third week. Neither he nor

Hunter had brought up the fact that the one-week time limit had expired. They both seemed to be intentionally overlooking it.

Because of the ground rules she'd established, all their time together hadn't been in the bedroom. They were doing other things, activities he would not have bothered doing with a woman. In addition to movies, dinner and dancing, they'd taken walks in the park, gone to the zoo, tried mountain climbing…and he'd even made an appearance at church. During the course of that time he had gotten to know Hunter in ways he hadn't thought possible. He knew her likes, her dislikes, things she tolerated and things she considered not up for negotiation. Likewise, he'd opened himself up to her as well. He felt comfortable telling her about his days at the hospital, and he even let her in on the Steele brothers' early plans for their parents' fortieth wedding anniversary.

This morning before leaving her bed he had been able to put the final piece of the puzzle in place. Now he knew why she had gotten under his skin, why he'd let her stay there and why he hadn't been able to get her out of his system. And why with her he felt possessed by passion. Bottom line was that he had fallen in love with her.

He'd tried convincing himself it was only lust, but he knew that wasn't the case each and every time they made love. Now he fully understood how Galen, Eli and Jonas felt about the women they'd fallen in love with and married. And as hard as it was to believe, he had no problem being included in that group, mainly because he couldn't consider his life without Hunter as a part of it.

"Tyson, are you listening to me?"

He really hadn't been. "Sorry, what did you say?"

"I asked who she is."

Tyson had no problem giving his brother a name. "Hunter McKay."

Mercury lifted a brow. Tyson could tell from his brother's expression he was recalling the time Hunter's name had come up during one of their parents' Thursday night dinners.

"Well, I hope you have a good reason for what you're doing."

He met his brother's stare. "Trust me. I do."

After Mercury left, Tyson knew exactly what he needed to do. He pulled out his cell phone to place a call. "Hi, Mom. Would it be a problem to set out an extra place setting for dinner tonight? You will be happy to know I've found the woman who will be permanently filling one of those three empty spots at the table."

"The flowers are beautiful."

Hunter had to agree with Pauline. The huge bouquet of red roses that had been delivered to her that morning was simply beautiful. She didn't have to read the card to know that Tyson had sent them. They had gone over their one-week agreement and were now into a third. She figured their time together had come to an end and the flowers were his parting gift to her.

Before leaving her apartment this morning he'd asked if he could decide where they would go tonight.

She didn't have a problem with his request. He hadn't said where they would be going. All he'd said was to dress casual and be ready at six.

Then she had arrived at work to see the flowers sitting on her desk. It had been years since she'd received flowers and like she told Pauline they were simply beautiful, although their suspected meaning caused a pain in her heart.

After Pauline left Hunter's office she sat behind her desk and drew in a deep breath. She'd been hoping...

What? That like her, Tyson would continue to ignore that they'd gone beyond the week they were to spend together? That he would claim she still wasn't out of his system, that he still felt possessed by passion and wanted more time together? Maybe that's what she was hoping, but unfortunately, the flowers were a clear indication that he had gotten over her and was now ready to move on.

Once again she had fallen in love with a man who would never truly love her in return. Story of her life, it seemed. But she would get over it because whether Tyson realized it or not, these past three weeks had meant everything to her. They had reinforced her belief in herself and she owed that to him.

He had made every single day with him special. Instead of protesting about anything she'd had on their list for them to do, he had readily embraced every activity. Whether it was going out to dinner, movies, concerts or dancing, he didn't seem to have a problem being seen with her. He'd even kept his word to her mother and gone to church with her. And because they had sat together, more than one pair of curious eyes had been on them.

The buzzer on her desk sounded. "Yes, Pauline?"

"Dr. Steele is on the line."

"Thanks." Was he calling to cancel tonight? Had he figured there was no need to wait until later to end things between them?

"Yes, Tyson?"

"Have you had lunch yet?"

"No."

"Good. I'll pick you up in a few minutes. There's something I want you to see."

He sounded rather mysterious but she went along with him. "Okay."

She hung up her phone, wondering what Tyson wanted her to see.

"Where are we going?"

Tyson smiled over at Hunter. He figured she would be curious since he hadn't given her much information. They had left the Phoenix city limits and were now headed toward the outskirts of town. "I think I've mentioned my cousin Morgan Steele to you before."

"He's the one who's the mayor of Charlotte, right?"

"Yes. His wife, Lena, owns a real estate company that has expanded into several states, including this one. I hired her to find some property in the country for me."

Hunter raised a brow. "Why?"

"To build that house you designed for me."

She frowned. "Tyson, we both know why you had me draw up those plans."

"Do we?" He knew Hunter thought she had things figured out.

"Of course. That was just a part of your plan to seduce me."

"Was it?"

Her frown deepened. "Okay, Tyson. What kind of game are you playing?"

A smile touched his lips. "No game. What if I told you I was dead serious about those house plans?"

"That would be news to me. Until today you haven't mentioned those plans since I gave them to you over a month ago."

Tyson brought his car to a stop in front of a wooded piece of property. He looked over at her. "I guess you can say I was waiting for a good time to do so."

The male in him appreciated her outfit. Today she was wearing another dress and although it wasn't as short as he'd like, it still showed off her gorgeous legs.

He glanced out the car window. "This is the property Lena found for me. What do you think?"

Hunter glanced around. She thought the land was pretty nice and told him so. Even from the car she could see a view of the mountains. The drive hadn't been too far from town, which wouldn't make his commute to the hospital too much of a hassle. Once he got on the interstate it would be a straight shot and he could get to work probably within twenty minutes.

"It's twenty-five acres on a private road," he said, intruding into her thoughts. "Not another house around for at least ten miles, and I think I'll like the seclusion. There's a huge lake on the property and plenty of trees."

"I think you'll like the seclusion, too," she said, not missing the excitement in his voice.

He pushed the button to extend his seat back to stretch out his legs. "Any ideas how the house will fit on it?"

Hunter shrugged as she glanced out the window again. "It shouldn't be a problem if you face the front of your house to the east. That way your bedrooms can take advantage of the view of the lake and mountains from any window."

He nodded. "I'm thinking of increasing the square footage to add a few more bedrooms. When I marry and have children I want to make sure they have plenty of space."

Personally, Hunter thought the house she'd designed had more than enough space already. However, if he thought he needed more than that, it was his business. She tried dismissing from her mind that this was the first time he'd ever mentioned a wife and children. He'd claimed he had no interest in ever getting married. Even when he'd given her specifics for what he wanted in a home, the subject of a wife and children had never entered the equation. "You're the client," she said. "I can modify the plans any way you want."

"I hope I'm more than just a client to you, Hunter."

Hunter nibbled on her bottom lip, not sure how to address that comment. She couldn't help but remember the roses sitting on her desk and what they probably meant.

"Thanks for the roses, by the way."

"You're welcome. Glad you liked them."

She drew in a deep breath. Even now while sitting in a parked car in a secluded area she could feel the chemistry between them. It seemed over the past few weeks, instead of diminishing, their physical attraction had gotten stronger. That would probably account for why their lovemaking was even more intense every night.

Tyson claimed he wasn't playing games, but for some reason she felt that he was. She was about to tell him so when he said, "You didn't respond to what I said about me being more than a client to you."

She studied him and then decided to turn the tables on him. "My response depends on whether I'm more than an architect to you."

Tyson knew he could put her mind to rest about that and intended to do so. He wasn't sure how she felt about him, but he figured any woman who'd given him as much of herself as she had during the time they'd spent together had to feel something for him.

He reached out and took her hand. "Hunter, there's something I need to say."

She pulled her hand away from him. "You don't have to say anything. I got the message with the roses."

He raised a brow. "And just what message did you get?"

"That you want us to end things."

He didn't say anything for a minute, and then he asked, "And you got that message from me sending you roses?"

"I had an employee back in Boston years ago. When

her boyfriend broke up with her, instead of sending her a 'Dear Jane' letter, he sent her a dozen 'Dear Jane' roses."

"And you figured that's what I did?"

"Isn't it?"

"No. You're right about me wanting us to end things...at least, wanting to end this phase of our relationship. But only for a new beginning."

She nodded. "I get it. You want another week."

He chuckled. "No, Hunter. I want forever." Tyson watched her face and wasn't surprised when shock spread across her features. He was tempted to lean over and kiss it right off her face.

"Forever?"

He nodded, watching her closely. "Yes, forever."

She evidently wasn't sure they were on the same page, because she asked, "You mean forever as in till death do us part?"

He chuckled. "Yes, that pretty much sums it up."

She stared at him like he had suddenly developed some kind of mental problem. "Why?"

"That's easy to answer. Because I've fallen in love with you."

She continued to stare at him for a long moment and then she shook her head. "That's impossible."

"And why is it impossible?"

"B-because you're Tyson Steele."

"I know who I am."

She glared at him. "Need I remind you that you're a man who goes through women quicker than you change your socks?"

"Last time I looked you're the only woman I've been with in well over a month now. I told you that I hadn't desired another woman since that night I ran into you at Notorious."

"But our relationship has been only physical."

"I beg to differ. Think about what we've been doing for the past few weeks. What we've shared. I've enjoyed spending time with you and doing things that had nothing to do with the bedroom."

When she didn't say anything he added, "I appreciate the time that we've gotten to know each other. Now more than ever I know you're the woman I want in my life."

When she didn't say anything but continued to stare at him, he pressed on. "I know I've laid a lot on the table and you need time to take it all in. I also know you probably don't reciprocate my feelings but I feel strongly that one day you will."

Hunter could not believe the words Tyson had spoken. He loved her? Really loved her as much as she loved him? She tried hard to fight back tears. "But I already do," she said, swiping the tears that were determined to fall anyway.

"You do what?"

"Reciprocate your feelings. I love you, too, Tyson. I think I fell in love with you the first time we made love. You made me feel so special. Like a woman who was truly appreciated. But not in a million years did I think you would, or could, love me back. You have… shall we say, a history with women."

"Yes, I do. But you effectively destroyed that history. You're the only woman I want. The only woman I could and will ever love."

More than anything she wanted to believe him, but hadn't Carter told her that same thing? But then, hadn't she discovered that Tyson wasn't anything like Carter?

"Hunter, will you marry me?"

She blinked. "Marry you?"

He nodded. "Yes."

"But how can you be sure that I'm the woman you want to spend your life with?"

He smiled. "I'm sure. Trust me, I fought it. Marrying anyone was the last thing on my mind, but my dad was right."

"About what?"

"Jonas said Dad once told him that a smart man knows there's nothing wrong with falling in love if it's a woman you can't live your life without. And I can't live my life without you, Hunter."

She wanted so much to believe him. "But what about those other women?"

"They don't matter. Not one of them had me possessed by passion. But you do, Hunter. I believe a man knows he's run his course with other women when they no longer interest him and none of them is more important to him than the one he wants to wake up with every morning and make memories with forever. And that's you."

He paused a moment to clear his throat. "So, I'm asking again. Hunter McKay, will you marry me? Will you be the only woman in my life? The one to share this house I'm building for us here on this property? The only one I want to be the mother of my children? The only one I want to wear the name of Mrs. Tyson Steele?"

At that moment, numerous emotions ran through Hunter and she knew what her answer to him would be. He was the only man she wanted in her life as well. "Yes, Tyson. I will marry you."

A huge smile curved Tyson's lips and he leaned over and captured her mouth with his. Shivers raced all through her body from the way his mouth was devouring hers. He was building passion neither of them could contain. And when he slid his arms around her waist to pull her over the console and into his lap, she followed his lead and returned the kiss with the same sexual hunger. Their tongues mated hotly, greedily. The degree of her desire for Tyson always astounded her, made her appreciate that she was a woman who wanted this man. And just to know he loved her as much as she loved him sent her soaring to the moon.

Moments later when the need to breathe overrode everything else, she pulled back from the kiss. He reached up and traced his finger across her moist lips. "I can sit here and kiss you all day," he said huskily.

"Umm, I prefer we do something else," she said leaning in to trail feathery kisses along the corners of his lips and chin.

"Something like what?"

"This," she said, climbing over his seat into the back and grabbing his hand to entice him to follow. He did. And then she shoved him on his back and straddled him.

"We can start here. We never got around to doing it in the backseat of your car eighteen years ago."

He chuckled softly as his hands grabbed hold of her thighs, easing her dress up nearly to her waist. "Back then you were a good girl."

"Now I'm bad," she said, pulling his zipper down. "Tyson's naughty girl."

"Soon to be his naughty wife," he said and then sucked in a deep breath when she reached inside his pants and took the solid thickness of his erection in her hand. When she began stroking him he released a guttural moan.

"You did say this is a private road, right?" she asked.

"Yes, it's very private."

"Good."

She opened her legs to cradle him and then remembered something. "Condom."

"Here," he said after working a packet out of his back pocket.

She took her time to sheathe him the way she'd seen him do many times. When he eased her panties aside she slid down, releasing a deep moan when the head of his erection touched her center just seconds before he tightened his hold on her hips and slowly entered her.

It was as if he was savoring the moment, though for her it was pure torture. She needed all of him now. She leaned in and bit him gently on the lips. In retaliation he thrust hard into her, melding their bodies.

"I thought that would get you going," she said, licking the mark her teeth had made on his lips.

Instead of responding he began moving, stroking her

insides, thrusting in and out, over and over again. Never had she felt so thoroughly made love to except for with Tyson. He had the ability to make her purr, yearn and become obsessed with everything he was doing to her.

"Hunter!"

When he screamed her name, she knew his world had tipped over the edge and hers would soon follow. He continued to stroke her while groaning out his pleasure. And she moaned, saying his name on a breathless groan, as the two of them were tossed into waves of pure ecstasy.

When Hunter found the energy to lift her head from his chest, she met his gaze. Their bodies were still intimately connected, and sexual chemistry, as explosive as it could get, still flowed between them the way it always did. A flirty smile touched her lips. "Let's do it again, Tyson," she said, leaning in close to lick the underside of his neck.

He smiled at her. "Yes, let's do it again. And then we'll go to the jewelry store for your engagement ring."

Epilogue

A beautiful day in August

Hunter couldn't stop looking down at the wedding ring Tyson had slid on her finger. It was beautiful. And then she glanced up at him. He was beautiful, as well.

"Tyson, will you repeat after me," the pastor said, reclaiming her attention. "With this ring, I thee wed."

Tyson held her gaze as he repeated the pastor's words loud and clear. She couldn't stop the tears from rolling down her cheeks. Mo and Kat would kill her for messing up a perfectly made-up face, but she couldn't help it. It was her wedding day and she could cry if she wanted to.

"By the power vested in me by this great state of Arizona, I now pronounce you husband and wife. Tyson, you may kiss your bride."

She smiled as he pulled her into his arms, sealing their vows with a kiss. When he released her he swept her off her feet as the pastor introduced them. "Dr. and Mrs. Tyson Steele."

As he carried her out the church while holding her in his arms, somewhere in the audience Hunter heard a voice say, "Another Bad News Steele bites the dust."

She tightened her arm around Tyson's neck, grateful that this particular Steele was hers.

Tyson tried to keep the smile off his face as he spoke with his brothers. "We're happy for you, man," Gannon said. "Hunter is wonderful."

"I think she's wonderful, too." He glanced over at Mercury. "Sorry, but the heat is going to be on you two guys. Maybe it won't be so bad since Eli and Stacey announced they are having a baby. That might keep Mom occupied for a while."

Mercury chuckled. "We can only hope. And I agree with Gannon. Hunter is great for you. She makes you happy and we can see it."

"Yes, I'm a very happy man." Tyson took a sip of his wine while glancing around Hunter's parents' beautifully decorated backyard. He and Hunter had decided on an outdoor wedding with only family and close friends. He saw his wife of one hour standing in a group talking to the wives of his cousins from Charlotte.

It was time for their first dance together as husband and wife. "Excuse me, guys."

He headed across the patio and as if she sensed his approach, Hunter glanced up and met his gaze. She smiled, excused herself from the group and met him halfway.

"Dr. Steele."

"Mrs. Steele. Ready for our first dance together?" he asked, taking her hand in his.

"Yes, I am ready."

"The sooner we can start our honeymoon the better," he said. They would be flying to Aruba, where they would spend the next two weeks.

"You sound rather anxious."

"I'll show you how anxious I am once I strip you naked," he said, leading her to the area designated for the dance floor.

Hunter lifted her head from Tyson's chest as they shared their first dance as husband and wife. "I never wanted to marry again, Tyson, but you made me change my mind about that."

He smiled down at her. "And I didn't want to ever marry but I was a man possessed and I couldn't do anything about it, sweetheart. You stole my heart before I knew what was happening."

She couldn't help but be filled with love for this man, who continued to show her what true love was about. He was the one who went out of his way to make her feel that she was everything a woman should be. Worthy of his love. Hunter couldn't help but remember that day they'd made love in the backseat of his car. Afterward, he had taken her to Lola's, one of the most exclusive jewelers in Phoenix. Together they had selected her engagement ring—a beautiful four-carat cushion diamond with a halo setting—as well as their diamond band wedding rings.

That evening he had surprised her by taking her to his parents' home to take part in the family's Thursday night dinner. Tyson's parents and the rest of the family had congratulated them, and of course the women had fallen in love with her engagement ring. Dinner had been special and since that night she'd been included in the Steeles' Thursday night dinners. She loved his parents and loved getting to know all of Tyson's brothers, as well as their wives.

"What are you thinking about, sweetheart?" Tyson asked, leaning down to whisper close to her ear.

"I was thinking just what a lucky woman I am."

"I feel lucky as well. You are everything I could ever want, Hunter."

He pulled her closer into his arms. He couldn't wait to be in their new home, dancing in their own backyard. Already the property had been cleared and construction had begun. According to the builder, they should be ready to move into their dream home in about six months.

"There are only two single Steeles now," Hunter observed, seeing Mercury and Gannon standing in a group talking with their cousins from Charlotte.

"I know, and I can't wait to meet the women who make them believe in a forever kind of love," Tyson said. "They're going to find out the same thing I did. You can't run from love."

Then he leaned down and captured her mouth with his, ignoring the claps and catcalls from their audience. When he released her mouth, she pulled in a deep breath. "What was that for?"

He chuckled. "Don't you know, baby? I am a man possessed. Not only am I possessed by your passion, I'm also possessed by your love."

Hunter sank closer into her husband's embrace and smiled up at him. "And I'm possessed by yours."

* * * * *